DOCTOR WHO AND THE SONTARAN EXPERIMENT

Based on the BBC television serial *The Sontaran Experiment* by Bob Baker and Dave Martin by arrangement with the British Broadcasting Corporation

IAN MARTER

Number 56 in the Doctor Who Library

D0931956

TARGET

A TARGET BOOK
published by
the Paperback Division of
W. H. ALLEN & Co. Ltd

A Target Book
published in 1978
by the Paperback Division of
W. H. Allen & Co. Ltd
A Howard & Wyndham Company
44 Hill Street, London W1X 8LB

Reprinted 1982 (twice)
Reprinted 1984

Printed and bound in Great Britain by
Cox & Wyman Ltd, Reading

ISBN 0 426 20049 7

Contents

I

Stranded

A huge red sun hung in the sulphurous yellow sky, its angry light filtering through thin clouds of whitish mist which swirled over the deserted, wasted landscape. Its dulled rays were reflected with a sinister glow in the scarred surfaces of nine spheres—each about a metre in diameter—which formed a perfect circle roughly twelve metres across.

The circle was set in an area of almost geometrical furrows and deep ruts, with blackened rocks showing through the scanty covering of dry, stringy, reed-like vegetation. The metallic skins of the nine globes were corroded and peeling, but here and there flickered a distorted image of the barren surroundings: rolling moorlands bristling with reddish ferns that rustled ceaselessly with an eerie, brittle sound; enormous rocky outcrops twisted into weird, nightmare shapes casting their monstrous shadows whenever the sun broke through the curling wraiths of vapour; and in the distance, massive cliffs hundreds of metres high with squarish, almost man-made outlines. The dry air stirred with warm and chilly breezes blowing together. Otherwise all was still.

Suddenly something loomed in the centre of the

circle of spheres. For a moment a bulky shape with a pale yellow light flashing above it wobbled uncertainly in the drifting mist. Then it abruptly vanished, leaving a dark, box-shaped hole. Seconds later it reappeared, accompanied by a raucous groaning sound which gradually died away like distant thunder. This time the pulsing light shone brilliantly and the ghostly object grew more distinct. It hovered, swaying precariously, then dropped heavily into the crackling reeds, coming to rest at a steep angle. The light was extinguished and silence fell.

Then excited human voices came from inside the shabby, blue-painted structure and several shadows moved across the frosted glass windows ranged along the top of each of its four sides. Painted above each row of windows were the words:

POLICE Public Call BOX

The chipped and weathered panelling of the 'box' creaked loudly as it swayed alarmingly to and fro, and it all but toppled over when a door suddenly flew open in the uppermost side. A very tall man appeared, balanced for a moment on the threshold, then took a deep breath and jumped lightly to the ground. He was dressed in a voluminous rust-coloured velvet jacket and oatmeal tweed trousers, and he wore an enormously long multi-coloured scarf tied with a giant knot under his chin. A battered felt hat with a wide brim was crammed haphazardly on top of his mass of brown curly hair. He surveyed the scene with a single sweep of his huge, eager blue eyes. Then, gathering up the trailing ends of the scarf, he strode across to the nearest silver sphere.

'What an extraordinary coincidence,' he boomed, kneeling down to examine the blistered metal. 'I wonder if it works.' Tugging an old-fashioned ear-trumpet from a bulging pocket, he clapped the battered horn against the globe and slowly moved it about while listening intently into the earpiece. He rapped on the sphere a few times with his knuckles and listened again. After a few seconds he sprang up, darted to the neighbouring globe and repeated his examination.

'I don't believe it,' he cried, springing up again and rushing across to examine a globe on the opposite side of the circle. Meanwhile a burly young man in duffle-coat and wellingtons had clambered out of the Police Box and was reaching up into the tilted door-way to help a trim young lady, clad in bright yellow waterproofs and sou'wester, to jump down.

All at once, with a noise like a sudden gust of wind, the Police Box vanished and the astounded young man found himself supporting his companion in mid-air. He stared open-mouthed at the black hole before his astonished eyes.

'Doctor ... What's happened to the TARDIS?' the girl cried.

'Quiet, Sarah,' commanded the kneeling figure: he had prised open a panel in the underside of the globe and was groping about inside it with a frown of concentration.

'But it ... it's gone!' Sarah cried, waving her arm about in front of her. 'It's just disappeared ...'

The Doctor glanced up irritably. Then he sprang to his feet. 'Harry—you've been meddling again,' he said angrily.

'But I haven't touched a thing,' Harry protested, promptly disappearing so that Sarah was left suspended above the ground for an instant before falling spreadeagled into the reeds. A few seconds later he re-appeared. 'Have I, Sarah?' he blinked and instantly vanished again. Sarah scrambled to her feet and looked in all directions for the invisible Harry.

'It's quite true, Doctor,' she grudgingly agreed. 'Just for once it's not Harry's fault ...' and she was almost knocked sideways as Harry re-appeared for the second time. 'Look, I do wish you would make up your mind, Harry,' she snapped, clinging to Harry's arm for support. He stared at her in a daze and mumbled his apologies.

'Quick, come out of the circle,' the Doctor shouted, waving his arms urgently. 'If this little lot should happen to get into phase at once you'll be gone forever,' and with that he dived back under the globe and resumed his investigation. 'You all right, old thing?' Harry asked, gallantly helping Sarah across the uneven area enclosed by the strange glinting spheres. Sarah shook herself free from Harry's grasp.

'In the first place I am not a *thing*,' she muttered through clenched teeth, stumbling over what looked like a mass of giant, petrified tree roots, 'and in the second place I am perfectly capable of fending for myself, thank you.'

'Excellent. I see you've decided to stay after all,' grinned the Doctor, glancing up as they joined him. He adjusted the settings on the handle of his sonic screwdriver—a complex instrument shaped like a pocket torch—and then reached up inside the sphere.

'I am afraid we've lost the TARDIS for the present,' he murmured, apparently fiddling with some kind of mechanism, 'but this is the most extraordinary piece of luck.'

Sarah looked at the ring of globes doubtfully. 'What is it for?' she asked. 'Losing the TARDIS doesn't seem very lucky to me.' She thrust her hands into the pockets of her luminous anorak and stared gloomily at Harry.

The Doctor emerged from the opening in the sphere and sat back on his heels. He tapped the side of the globe and made it vibrate like a gong. Harry jumped.

'This is an old Tri-Phasic Triple Field design,' the Doctor cried with enthusiasm, 'but it appears to be virtually intact, and I think that, with a little effort, I can almost certainly get it to work.'

'Yes, Doctor, but what is it *for*?' Sarah repeated.

'It's an early prototype matter transmitter, of course,' the Doctor said. 'As soon as I get these nine little beasts into phase, we should be able to retrieve the TARDIS and then pop back up to the Terra Nova and tell Vira that all is well.'

Sarah backed away a few paces with a wary glance around the circle, her recent experiences with such devices still vivid in her mind.

Harry stared incredulously at the Doctor. 'You

11

mean Vira's people are going to use these overgrown ball-bearings to reach Earth?' he cried.

'Precisely, Harry,' grinned the Doctor, and he darted along to the next globe and got to work with ear trumpet, sonic screwdriver and magnifying glass.

'Well, they'll have quite a job to build themselves a new world here,' Sarah muttered, shivering slightly in a sudden swirl of mist and glancing up apprehensively at the great red sun. Harry stared at the inhospitable, scorched terrain stretching emptily around them.

'Where . . . where exactly are we anyway?' he asked.

'I set the Orientators for Piccadilly Circus,' came the Doctor's muffled reply, 'but since this little machine seems to have kidnapped us . . .'

'. . . We could be just about anywhere,' Sarah chimed in with a sigh. There was a pause while the Doctor, grunting with exertion and muttering away to himself, continued with his delicate adjustments.

'Oh, come on, Harry,' Sarah suddenly said with an impulsive toss of her head, 'let's go and find Nelson's Column,' and she set off through the crackling reeds. Harry hesitated for a moment or two and then followed.

'Might as well have a little recce,' he agreed.

'I think you'll find that Trafalgar Square is more in *that* direction,' came a muffled call. They turned: the Doctor's head and shoulders were hidden inside the globe he was repairing, but one long arm was sticking out like a signpost and pointing in the opposite direction to the way they were heading.

Following the Doctor's finger, Sarah and Harry looked towards a broad, shallow valley covered in a thick tangle of reeds and dry ferns, where the mist hung in mysterious dense patches. They shrugged and set off again in the direction the Doctor indicated. As they began to descend through the undergrowth, stumbling among the concealed rocks and boulders, a distant voice behind them called, 'Do mind the traffic . . .'

His natural curiosity getting the better of him with every step, Harry was soon leading the way down into a deep gorge, its steep sides covered in strange kinds of moss which resembled mouldy bread, and in rubbery, fungus-like growths the colour of burnt toffee. Enormous, rocky outcrops reared above them like fantastic heads carved out of ebony, and all around them were scattered massive glassy boulders. Here and there rattled patches of reed and thickets of giant thorn bristled with vicious reddish daggers. Harry searched eagerly about in the undergrowth and among the treacherous crevasses which ran in all directions, exclaiming with delight and surprise at each unfamiliar sign of organic life he found.

'I say, old thing, look at these,' he cried, reaching up towards a cluster of gigantic berries growing in a cleft. Sarah glanced at the shrivelled black fruits and shuddered. She was becoming more and more apprehensive: while Harry had forged on ahead, she had been holding back and looking cautiously around her. Once or twice she was sure that she heard leathery flapping sounds high in the mists, and she was rapidly becoming convinced that hidden eyes were fixed on them from all sides.

'Don't touch them, Harry,' she murmured.

'Sarah ... whatever's the matter?' he exclaimed.

Sarah stopped. 'I don't like it, Harry,' she said, 'it's not like Earth at all.'

'But it's quite fantastic,' cried Harry, squeezing one of the poisonous-looking berries. A treacly green juice burst out over his fingers. 'These botanic mutations are ...'

'Mutations!' Sarah gasped, her eyes widening. Harry nodded and held out his hand to show the rubbery green globules clinging to his fingers. 'The result of unnaturally high solar radiation levels, I expect,' he explained casually.

Sarah looked up into the drifting veils of vapour. 'Harry ... there's something up there,' she whispered. Harry put his arm reassuringly around her shoulders.

'Nonsense,' he laughed, glancing upwards. 'I don't suppose any of our feathered friends survived.' He gave Sarah a comforting squeeze and wandered away up towards the head of the ravine.

'Mind you,' he went on, 'some of the Reptiles might have managed.'

Sarah followed, reluctant, but anxious to keep up. 'You mean there might be ... well ... *things* here?' she called softly. Harry shrugged.

'There can't have been any animal life on Earth— not of any size—for thousands of years,' he replied, reaching the brow of the rocky slope. 'But things will change when Vira and her people arrive—their Animal/Botanic Section was chock-a-block with ...'

Harry's words died abruptly and he seemed to suddenly disappear into the ground. Her heart thumping, Sarah was rooted to the spot. She waited for Harry to pick himself up, but nothing happened. She edged forward very slowly. All at once, a flurry of clattering and flapping noises burst from a nearby outcrop above her. She peered fearfully up at the misty slopes but could see nothing. The gorge echoed a moment, and then went quiet.

Sarah crept cautiously over the slippery rocks, glancing constantly behind her. Just as she began to climb the slope leading to the spot where Harry had been swallowed up, a hail of pebbles suddenly rattled down into the ravine and bounced violently around her. She stared wildly upwards. A dark shape hung momentarily in a thin patch of mist and then vanished with a leathery clatter. Gasping with terror, Sarah started to scramble recklessly over the uneven ground. Just before she reached the brow she slipped and pitched forward with a scream. She glimpsed a huge black space yawning in front of her like a monstrous mouth, and then everything exploded as she cracked her head on a boulder.

The Doctor had shed his hat and scarf and was now busily tinkering with the fifth globe in the circle of nine: testing and repairing circuits and re-designing whole sections of the intricate, compact mechanism. The work was progressing well and he was whistling jolly tunes softly to himself. He had become so absorbed in the task that he had forgotten all about Sarah Jane Smith and Surgeon-Lieutenant Harry

Sullivan RN almost as soon as they had set off. He was quite oblivious to the low, persistent humming sounds which came and went with the wind above the rustling of the reeds, and totally unaware that he was being closely watched.

Concealed in the twisted and furrowed rocks thrusting through a nearby patch of dense reeds, two men were lying full length and observing the Doctor's activities with hostile eyes. One of them squinted through the sights of a short, rifle-like weapon which was trained on the unsuspecting figure kneeling beside the sphere. Both men were dressed in protective suits made from a heavy plastic material, with helmet anchorages around the collars. The remains of thick gloves fluttered on their scarred, dirty hands and the suits were ripped and filthy. The men's hair and beards were matted and their faces pale with dulled, bloodshot eyes ringed with fatigue.

After a while, one of them stirred.

'Keep him covered, Zake,' he muttered hoarsely. 'I'll get the others.'

His companion stretched the cramp out of his arms. 'Right, Krans,' he murmured, 'but be careful. The Scavenger's been nosing around a bit too close for comfort today.' Zake peered closely into the sights, his eyes narrowing with hatred. 'And hurry,' he added, 'I can't wait to get my hands on this one.' Krans grunted ominously and, keeping his big body crouched low, slid away down into the reeds and was gone.

For a long time Zake lay hidden in the rocks, the

ion gun trained carefully on the Doctor's back. From time to time he spat into the reeds and muttered, 'We've got you at last ... we've got you now.' Then suddenly he stiffened. A relentless humming noise was quickly approaching, its sound rising and falling like a siren. Sweat broke out all over Zake's body and ran into his eyes. His skin prickled with fear as he listened, his eyes still hypnotised by the Doctor's crouching figure. He licked his dry, cracked lips and waited.

The humming steadied behind him. At first he could not move. All at once he twisted round with a gasp and struggled to aim the weapon with trembling hands at the object hovering in the air above the blackened rocks. The scanner lens bore into his face with its cold electronic stare, and quiet clicking sounds came from inside its domed metal body. Zake leaped up and, diving underneath the hovering robot, stumbled blindly into the reeds and down the hillside. Humming and chattering to itself, the robot glided in pursuit. Desperately Zake ran for his life, hampered by the heavy flapping suit and thick boots. Again and again he turned and fired the ion gun at point-blank range. The invisible stream of ionised particles was absorbed harmlessly by the robot's metallic surface. Relentlessly it pursued him and Zake realised that his plight was hopeless.

He veered sharply into a deep gully, frantically seeking some small niche or hole where he could take refuge and where the robot could not penetrate. As he turned, a whip-like metal tentacle flashed through the air and wound itself tightly round his neck like a noose. He was jerked sharply off his feet with a sickening crunch. His piercing scream was instantly transformed into a hideous, throttled gasp as he fell and lay absolutely still among the reeds. The robot hovered motionless for a few moments, chattering quietly away to itself. Then it uncoiled its tentacle and withdrew it with a snap, gliding smoothly away into the mist.

Zake's stifled scream had brought the Doctor leaping to his feet. 'Harry!' he breathed, dropping the delicate circuits which he had been sonic-soldering into the undergrowth. Snatching up his hat and scarf he set off at a loping run towards the rocky knoll.

Sarah came to after a few seconds and found herself staring down into a deep, dark hole three or four metres across with sheer rocky sides. In a daze she gripped the crumbling edge a few centimetres in front of her face, dislodging a shower of sharp fragments which clattered in the gloom below.

'Hey, watch out, old thing,' called Harry's anxious voice. 'I don't fancy being buried alive, you know.'

Sarah clutched her splitting head, almost sobbing with relief. 'Harry!' she cried. 'I can't see you. Are you badly hurt?' She heard furious scrambling sounds from the bottom of the hole.

'Hardly a scratch, old thing,' Harry replied, 'I was very lucky ... All the same,' he went on, 'I don't see how I can climb out of here. I seem to be trapped.'

Sarah glanced round, vainly searching for something to use as a ladder or rope. Then she suddenly noticed the collapsed remains of a carefully constructed camouflage of reeds and foliage through which Harry had fallen.

'There's something funny here, Harry,' she murmured, struggling to clear her aching head.

'It may appear highly comical to *you*, Miss Smith,' Harry muttered testily, 'but I'm afraid I don't see ...'

'Harry, this hole was deliberately covered over,' Sarah interrupted with a frown. Harry snorted with exasperation.

'Well of course it was,' he cried, 'otherwise I wouldn't have fallen down ... Oh, I see what you mean,' he added after a pause, 'a deliberate trap, eh?'

For a moment Sarah said nothing. For all her fear, her journalistic instinct was beginning to scent a good story. 'Man-traps ... on an uninhabited planet?' she murmured at last.

'What did you say?' came Harry's muffled voice from the darkness.

Sarah pulled herself together. 'I'm going to fetch the Doctor,' she said firmly.

'Yes ... well ... I'll just stay here then,' Harry called plaintively after her.

Sarah took a deep breath, stuck out her chin resolutely, and slipped away into the echoing ravine.

The Doctor looked down at Zake's crumpled body. He was greatly relieved to find that it was not Harry or Sarah.

19

'Broken neck, poor fellow,' he murmured, gently closing the lids over the wild, dead eyes. He remained for a moment staring thoughtfully at the dead man's space-suit, then he sprang up and made towards the top of the outcrop, filled with apprehension for the safety of his two missing companions. But just as he emerged from the narrow gully, something seized him from behind and tightened round his throat so that he could scarcely breathe. At the same instant a huge figure, clad in a space-suit identical to that of the dead man, dropped from a ledge in front of him, barring the way.

The Doctor was forced to his knees, choking and gasping, his eyes bulging out of his head. His hair was grabbed and his head wrenched viciously back. The scarf bit into his neck.

'You killed our mate ... You killed Zake,' growled the powerful figure standing over him.

'And now we've got *you*,' rasped a second voice behind him.

The Doctor fought to loosen the suffocating noose. 'I do assure you ... I have no intention ... of hurting anyone ...' he gasped. 'Please ... please, release me ...'

'Just try convincing the others,' sneered the towering figure, and again the Doctor's head was jerked sharply back.

'We've all waited a long time for this,' the voice behind him threatened in an ominous undertone.

Unable to speak, the Doctor tried to twist round to face the hidden captor but his head was thrust violently forward again. The giant figure loomed larger and larger as the Doctor stared, until it seemed to fill the sky. Then he lost consciousness.

2

Unknown Enemies

Sarah eventually found her way back to the ghostly circle of glinting spheres, after a breathless and spine-chilling scramble through the alien landscape. All around her the mist gathered itself into massive, haunting shapes, and the enormous red eye of the sun followed her with its inescapable malevolent gaze. At every turn she was pursued by the leathery flapping sounds which seemed to stop whenever she paused to listen and peer about, but instantly continued as soon as she pressed desperately onward.

The circle was deserted. The Doctor was nowhere to be seen. Sarah searched frantically in all directions, calling until she was hoarse. Then she stumbled upon the pieces of circuitry the Doctor had dropped, and nearby she found the sonic screwdriver hidden among the reeds. She stared at the scattered mechanism, filled with foreboding.

'Oh, Doctor . . .' she murmured, 'what's happened?'

A faint humming sound began to approach in the distance. Clutching the sonic screwdriver tightly, Sarah crouched down behind one of the globes and strained to see through the drifting mist. She thought she could just make out a greenish glow in the air among some jagged rocks half a kilometre away. It was coming slowly towards the circle. Sarah sprang up and began to run, tripping and stumbling, towards the ravine where Harry lay trapped. Feeling utterly alone and helpless, she tore through the snapping reeds and over the treacherous rocks, with the flapping and the humming noises gaining on her at every stride.

Harry groped cautiously round his dark prison. He shuddered as his hands touched razor-sharp edges and spikes of rock.

'Lucky I wasn't sliced to mincemeat,' he murmured ruefully. Gradually, his eyes accustomed themselves to the gloom and he saw that he had fallen into a deep fault in the rock. Fortunately, the criss-cross camouflage of reeds had broken his fall and he had escaped with a few cuts and bruises. Far above him the mist curled round the crooked edges of the opening. He quickly realised that he had no hope of climbing the sheer twisting sides back to the surface. He would just have to wait until Sarah returned with the Doctor, and hope that the Doctor could devise some clever method to rescue him.

The air down in the fissure was curiously warm and it smelt like a mixture of sulphur and hot oil. Harry quickly discovered that warm air was issuing from narrow shaft-like openings scattered around the sides of the hole. He considered trying to wriggle into one of them to see if it might lead him back up to the surface, but the warm fumes made him think of volcanoes and the unknown depths of the Earth. He was afraid even to put his arm into one of the openings.

He was about to investigate a cluster of strange bubble formations in the floor of the cavernous fault, when something flew past his face and shattered one of the globules as if it were made of glass. Harry reeled backwards, his face stinging from the impact of dozens of tiny, sharp fragments. Then a cascade of stones ricochetted around him. Harry shielded his face with his arms and peered cautiously but expectantly upward.

'Sarah?' he called. 'Is that you?' Another fusillade of missiles careered down and shattered in a series of bursts behind him. 'Hey ... Steady on, old thing,' he yelled, cradling his head and crouching against the wall of the cavern.

There was a brief lull. Harry listened, full of misgiving. The only sound from above was a strange flapping, and what seemed like laboured breathing which came and went round the edge of the hole far above him.

'Look here,' he began, venturing slowly to his feet. Just in time he jammed himself into the nearest of the narrow openings as a sudden hail of boulders, pebbles and dust started to fly around the crevasse. As the roaring avalanche increased, Harry forced himself further and further into the tunnel. For a few agonising moments he was faced with a choice: either to risk being crushed alive under the rocks, in the hope of eventual rescue; or to brave whatever horrors might lie in wait inside the tunnel. Even as he hesitated, the entrance of the shaft was rapidly blocked with boulders and splinters of rock. He no longer had any choice; there was only one way he could go.

The Doctor's limp body was dumped at the entrance to a small cave let into the base of a towering cliff-face and overlooking a vast plain scored with deep canyons. The mouth of the cave was half covered by a crude awning of reeds and thick ferns, and nearby, an open fire blazed fiercely.

A scruffily bearded, wiry man dressed in the remains of a heavy space-suit unwound the scarf from the Doctor's neck and rapidly bound his arms tightly to his sides. The massive figure of Krans emerged from the cave carrying a small flask. He flung some of the contents into the Doctor's face with a mumbled curse.

'Are you mad, Krans?' cried the other man, trying to snatch the container away. 'I don't want to die of thirst yet: not until I have to.'

Krans brushed him aside with a shrug of his power-ful shoulder. 'He's coming round, Erak,' he growled. The Doctor's eyes had flickered open and then closed again.

Krans lumbered over to the fire and drew out a crackling branch which he brought over and thrust towards the Doctor's face. 'What have you done with the rest of our crewmates?' he snarled.

The Doctor flinched away from the blazing brand

with a gasp. He opened his eyes and looked down at his pinioned arms with a mildly puzzled expression. Then he stared straight at Krans and smiled. 'Do you think I could have a glass of water?' he croaked. Krans pushed the burning branch closer. The Doctor pressed himself back against the cliff.

'What's happened to Roth and Warra and Henk ...?' snapped Erak.

The Doctor craned round to look at him. 'Oh dear,' he sighed, 'I was so hoping for news of some dear friends of my own ... but I fear I cannot help *you* at all.'

'So there are more of you,' said a clear, authoritative voice from beyond the makeshift porch. A tall, slim, fair-haired man of about forty was gazing contemptuously at the Doctor's bound, huddled figure.

'Two very dear companions,' said the Doctor, struggling to sit more upright. 'Perhaps *you* have seen them?'

'Where did you find him?' demanded the newcomer, ignoring the Doctor.

'First saw him lurking around that damned circle,' Erak replied, giving the Doctor a sharp nudge so that he fell sideways, unable to save himself.

'I was not lurking,' he corrected gently, 'I was simply attempting to repair that old Transmat Installation when I ...'

Erak jerked the Doctor upright again.

'That old *what*?' cried the tall newcomer, approaching with an incredulous stare.

'There's no Transmat here,' Erak snapped. 'The Earth's been junked.'

26

The Doctor shook his head emphatically. 'Temporarily abandoned perhaps,' he smiled, 'but far from "junked" as you call it.'

'It's finished ... useless ...' Krans shouted in a sudden burst of fury. 'It's nowhere near the Patrol Zones ... So no one comes here, ever. Check, Vural?' Krans flung his last remark up at the tall, fair-haired man. He nodded slowly in agreement.

'How did you get here?' Vural demanded, staring down at the Doctor.

'I was about to ask you the same question,' the Doctor replied calmly, his eyes watering with the smoke from the glowing branch. Krans suddenly shoved it right up against the Doctor's face, quivering with pent-up violence.

'Don't play smart with us,' he hissed. Then he turned to Vural. 'We're getting nowhere like this,' he muttered. 'So why don't we finish him off?'

Vural motioned Krans to lay off. He fixed the Doctor with piercing eyes and said in a quiet but menacing tone, 'You know well enough how we got here. We were in orbit, measuring Solar Radiation levels. You sent out a bogus Mayday Call and enticed us down here. When we left the Scout to look around, the ship was vapourised. Nine of us are stranded.'

The Doctor glanced around, his face creased with pain from the livid burn on his cheek.

'Where are the others?' he asked, through clenched teeth.

There was a short pause. Then Vural spoke. 'Your Scavenger got them.'

The Doctor stared up at the tall figure in front of

27

him. 'My what?' he murmured, his eyes widening.

When at last Sarah reached the pit she was almost hysterical with fear. The invisible humming pulsated softly somewhere in the ravine behind her. She sank down with aching lungs at the edge of the hole and called down into the darkness, 'Harry ... the Doctor's completely disappeared. I just can't find him anywhere.' There was no reply and no movement from below. Sarah peered anxiously through the smashed and scattered reeds. 'Harry, what are we going to do?' she cried. She was aware of the humming coming slowly nearer and nearer behind her. Then she caught sight of the mass of fallen rock lying in the bottom of the pit. 'Harry ... What's happened ... Where are you?' she screamed.

Sarah spun round. A strange greenish light was approaching along the foot of the ravine. She seized a dead branch—like a length of bamboo—from the shattered camouflage. Wielding it in front of her like a club, she backed away from the eerie, humming glow towards a group of enormous boulders, her wellingtons slithering perilously close to the edge of the gaping hole beside her. Just as she felt her back against the nearest boulder, a rapid panting and flapping burst out among the rocks behind her. She tried to turn round but she found herself hypnotised by the quivering glow gliding smoothly towards her.

The panting came nearer. Sarah felt warm breath on the back of her neck. She gave a start, and lost her footing on the crumbling edge. Her cry of horror was stifled by a large, gloved hand, as she was lifted bodily and carried away among the boulders. She tried to twist round, but her captor held her like a vice. A few seconds later, a dome-shaped object, the size of a very large bell, glided up out of the mist and hovered humming over the yawning pit. Its metallic surface bristled with antennae and probes, and was studded with small covered apertures. The air surrounding the machine formed an iridescent haze.

Sarah stopped struggling and stared in fascination as a thin tentacle emerged from one of the apertures and snaked down into the hole where it seemed to grope for something. There was a pause while the robot clicked softly to itself, and then the tentacle was retracted. A mechanism like a periscope containing a large lens began to sweep the area around the pit. Sarah's head was forced down between the boulders, out of sight, but she could hear the machine emit a series of shrill bleeping sounds and then glide away, out of the ravine.

When the humming had faded into the distance, Sarah was abruptly released. A tall, gaunt figure in a ragged space-suit flapped past her and moved cautiously into the open to check that the robot had gone. With fearful backward glances, it loped back to where Sarah was crouching among the rounded, glassy rocks. The rubbery slapping of the ripped material sent a shiver through her body.

'So it was *you* following me—making that noise,' she said, with a mixture of relief and suspicion.

Sarah found herself face to face with a terrified, trembling individual with cropped black hair, a thin beard and dark, almost Oriental features. His face was emaciated and covered in barely-healed scars.

'Who are you?' he whispered. 'Where are you from?'

'Just what I was going to ask *you*,' Sarah blurted, relaxing a little. 'My name is Sarah. I come from Earth—but it's rather a long story, I'm afraid.'

The man stared at her for several minutes, mouthing the unfamiliar name. 'I am Roth,' he said at last.

Sarah's courage began to return. She managed a smile. 'Do you live here ... on Earth?' she asked. Roth shook his head sharply, indicating his tattered space-suit. When he moved his arms, the torn material flapped noisily—like bats' wings. Sarah swallowed hard.

'Tell me about the machine,' she said tentatively. 'Why are you afraid of it?'

Roth gaped at her in disbelief. 'Do you not know?' he whispered. Sarah shook her head. Roth wrung his gloved hands together and an almost crazed expression came into his eyes. 'That ... that is the Scavenger,' he gasped. Sarah shuddered. It seemed suddenly to have grown colder.

'What is it for?' she murmured.

'It catches us,' Roth cried, staring wildly about. 'It captures my crewmates and takes them ... for torture.' Sarah clutched her anorak closer to her.

'Where does it take them?' she asked. Roth pointed in the direction the machine had taken.

30

'To the Alien,' he muttered.

Sarah's eyes widened. 'What Alien?' she breathed.

'In the rocks ... the thing in the rocks ...' Roth cried, his voice breaking with panic. Suddenly Sarah noticed the horrific burn marks showing through the tears in Roth's suit.

'Did the Alien do that to you?' she asked gently.

Roth nodded, covering his wounds. 'It killed Warra and Henk,' he mumbled, 'but I got away ... yunnerstan?' Roth cowered beside Sarah, shivering, his teeth chattering. 'I don't get caught again ... Not me.' He pointed to the pit in front of them. 'I made traps, and I'll get it ... soon ... you'll see ...' A sudden defiance blazed in Roth's eyes, and it gave Sarah renewed courage.

'Roth, you've got to help me,' she said earnestly. 'I came here with two friends and they have both vanished ... yunnerstan ...? I mean, you understand?' she corrected herself. Roth nodded furiously. 'I saw them ... I watched you,' he gabbled. 'One of them is at the camp ... with Vural. They found him at the circle.'

Sarah's face lit up. She grasped Roth's ragged sleeve. 'You mean you know where the Doctor is?' she cried.

Vural and his crew were rapidly losing patience with the Doctor. His calm politeness baffled them and deepened their suspicions. Krans was seething with the desire to avenge his murdered crewmates, and had to be forcibly restrained by Vural and Erak when

31

the Doctor quietly denied all knowledge of the Scavenger.

'I have already explained,' he was saying wearily, 'we arrived on Earth a short time ago, and we have temporarily mislaid our transport. As soon as I can complete my adjustments we can return to the Terra Nova.' There was a pause while the three crewmen stared at the Doctor.

'He's crazy,' spat Krans, giving the embers of the fire a vicious kick.

'You don't really expect us to believe that,' said Vural with an ironic smile.

'Why shouldn't you?' the Doctor asked innocently.

'Because the Terra Nova doesn't exist,' Krans sneered.

Vural gave a short laugh. 'The Lost Colony,' he said dismissively. 'It's a good story that mothers tell their children.'

The Doctor was leaning forward, secretly testing the tightness of his bonds. 'Fascinating,' he murmured, 'a myth ... like Atlantis ...'

'And it's never been found,' Erak said with menacing finality.

It was no good. Weakened as he was by his recent treatment at the hands of Krans and Erak, the Doctor knew he could not possibly free himself from the unyielding coils of the scarf. His only hope was to play for time. He had been observing something odd about Vural's manner, and it had given him an idea.

'Well, I can assure you that it was real enough when I left it,' he smiled with childlike frankness.

'The Earth's been cool a long time now,' Vural scoffed, 'and the Terra Novans have never come back.'

'But the survivors are re-awakening at this very moment,' the Doctor cried, looking round excitedly. 'They will be delighted to discover that they are not the sole remaining members of the human species.' His eyes fixed with a sudden frown upon a small object suspended like a pendant round Vural's neck, and just visible inside his open suit. He leaned forward as far as he could to look more closely.

'You *are* human, I take it,' the Doctor murmured. For a moment Vural hesitated. He glanced quickly down at his chest, and then furtively across at Krans and Erak. They were staring uncertainly at the Doctor.

Vural pushed him roughly back against the outer wall of the cave, and said rapidly, clutching the front of his suit together, 'Galsec Colony Seven.'

Slumped against the rock, his hat tipped over his forehead, the Doctor gazed searchingly at Vural through half-closed eyes. In a whisper that neither Krans nor Erak could hear, he said, 'Nevertheless, your little trinket is not a product of human technology, I fancy ...'

On the other side of the cliffs which towered above them lay a vast crater completely enclosed by the circular range of jagged crags. Hidden somewhere inside the crater was a brightly flickering fluorescent screen and for a few moments the Doctor's face had loomed there as a bulbous, distorted image, his piercing eyes staring out. Then something had blotted the image, and the screen had darkened.

At that moment, there had been a hissing intake of breath: a nightmare gasp of anger and frustration. Three enormous talons sheathed in a heavy, paw-like glove had hovered over the mass of switches clustered around the screen. Then the 'hand' had swept down and cut the picture with a vicious jab.

Sarah did her best to keep up as the agile Roth led her swiftly towards the Galsec Colonists' hideout. He leaped through gullies and over ridges as if he knew every single metre of the terrain. Suddenly he pulled her down into the reeds, and pointed towards the ragged cliff hanging nearby in the mist.

'Your friend ... the Doctor ... he's just aways up there,' he whispered.

'Come on then,' Sarah panted, promptly setting off. But Roth remained crouching in the undergrowth, the whites of his eyes showing starkly as he glanced sidelong towards the base of the cliff.

'What's the matter?' Sarah frowned, turning back. 'What is there to be afraid of—they're your mates.' Roth shook his head vehemently.

'Not Vural,' he muttered.

Sarah flinched away in alarm as Roth suddenly seized her arm fiercely, fixing her with a crazed stare.

'Vural's hooked,' he hissed. 'The Scavenger caught him ... took him to the crater ... but the Alien let him go ... I saw it.'

'But you must help me reach the Doctor,' Sarah pleaded, trying to free her arm. 'Perhaps the Doctor can help you against the Alien.' For a moment Sarah thought that Roth was going to go berserk. She wrenched herself away from him with a gasp. Then suddenly he grinned, pushing her gently in the direction of the cliff, and set off in a kind of frenzied dance, uttering wild shouts and waving his long arms in the air.

Krans paced restlessly in the entrance to the cave, gripping the ion gun in his big hands and muttering threats under his breath. Vural had recovered his composure and was closely questioning the Doctor in an attempt to trap him.

'All right,' he snapped, 'how long have the Terra Novans been in deep-freeze?'

'Perhaps fifteen thousand years ...' The Doctor shrugged, as far as his bonds would allow.

'And you woke up before the others,' scoffed Erak, taking a swig from the water-flask.

'No, no, no,' said the Doctor patiently. 'I just happened to find them in the nick of time. Earth has been habitable for a few centuries, but their clock stopped and they overslept.'

'Clock?' echoed Vural, his clenched fists like marble.

'Yes,' the Doctor went on, 'and since I am something of an expert where time is concerned, I just made a few ...'

With a lightening movement, like a jack-knife opening, the Doctor sprang to his feet, taking the

35

three Galsec crewman completely by surprise. 'I say,' he cried, jumping precariously onto a boulder, 'It's just occurred to me, I might well be able to help *you* —after all, you don't want to be marooned here for ever ...' Vural and Erak slowly advanced towards the Doctor, while Krans covered him with the ion gun. 'But first,' the Doctor chattered on, tensing like a panther about to spring, 'I'd like a couple of eggs lightly boiled and a slice or two of toast and honey ...'

At that moment, wild cries were heard in the distance. Erak whirled round. 'Look ... it's Rothy,' he cried, pointing into the valley. Vural and Krans turned and stared. Then all three began to run towards the weirdly capering figure of their lost crewmate. When Roth saw them approaching he streaked away, zig-zagging out of sight with the Doctor's three captors in hot pursuit.

No sooner had their cries died away, than Sarah slipped along the foot of the cliff and started feverishly tugging at the knotted scarf.

'Hallo, Sarah.' The Doctor grinned delightedly. 'Who's your speedy friend?'

'Explain later,' Sarah panted, freeing the Doctor's arms. 'Come on,' she cried, dragging him away along the cliff.

'Where are we going?' the Doctor shouted, clinging on to his hat.

'To the pit, of course,' Sarah cried impatiently.

'Wait!' the Doctor called anxiously. 'The sonic screwdriver ... I seem to have mislaid it ... I feel quite lost without it ...'

Sarah instantly produced the vital instrument from her pocket, and the Doctor seized it with a brilliant smile of relief. 'Now I'm ready for anything,' he beamed. 'Lead on MacSmith ...'

3

Capture

Sweat poured into Harry's eyes as he forced his way along the twisting, narrow tunnel, the roar of the avalanche still sounding in his ears. The shaft had soon turned upward at a steep angle, and now it was almost vertical. His thick duffle-coat afforded some protection against the treacherously sharp edges and nodules covering the inside of the shaft, but at the same time it seriously hampered Harry's progress, and once or twice he feared he would be completely jammed. Occasionally, he reached a slightly wider section where the rock surface seemed smoother—as if it had been polished—and he found himself suddenly beginning to slide down again. His elbows and knees were soon raw with the effort of working his way back upwards.

Here and there he encountered other, similar shafts branching off at all angles. Harry ignored these and struggled on towards what he hoped would prove to be the surface. The same warm, sulphurous breeze issued from all the tunnels making the air thick and suffocating, so that Harry's throat burned and his head throbbed. Whenever he paused for breath, curious distant sounds—like the pounding of machinery —reached his ears.

Eventually, something glinted far above him. Harry felt like cheering: it was daylight; it had to be daylight. He frantically redoubled his efforts, oblivious of the cuts and grazes on his hands and the stinging in his eyes and lungs.

But within seconds he realised that he was as far away from escape as ever. The shaft was steadily narrowing around him as he climbed. As it tapered more and more, he finally found himself completely stuck just within reach of safety. There seemed to be no way he could squeeze through the last couple of metres. Harry beat the sides of the tunnel in frustration, peering up at the tantalizingly close patch of sky from which the fresh air wafted down onto his burning face.

'If only I hadn't done all that rowing at medical school,' he muttered, giving a last, futile shrug of his muscular shoulders in the narrow aperture. For a few minutes he gratefully drank in the cool air from above. Then gingerly he began working his way downwards again. He would have to try one of the other branching shafts after all ...

The Doctor and Sarah Jane stood at the edge of the pit staring down at the tangle of boulders and branches in the half-light. The Doctor chewed thoughtfully on a reed.

'He couldn't just have climbed out,' Sarah said after a while.

The Doctor grunted. 'The machine you saw,

Sarah,' he murmured, 'could that have lifted Harry out?'

Sarah shook her head. 'He'd already disappeared when the machine came,' she explained.

Suddenly the Doctor bent down and picked up a small piece of metallic material, half-hidden in a patch of scrubby fern at the edge of the hole. He studied it intently. 'Your machine appears to be moulting, Sarah,' he muttered. 'What's more, it's made out of Terullian.'

'Is that significant?' asked Sarah.

'Very,' replied the Doctor frowning, and biting so hard on the reed that it snapped off and fell into the pit. 'It's an exceptionally rare kind of metal—half mineral and half organic—and it isn't found in this Galaxy at all . . . in fact, it is quite . . . quite . . .'

'Alien,' rasped a voice behind them, making them both jump. Sarah clutched the Doctor's arm in terror.

'Just the word I wanted,' cried the Doctor, recovering himself at once, and turning round with a grin. The crazed face of Roth was staring at them from among the nearby boulders. The Doctor advanced towards him with outstretched hand. 'A most efficient decoy, if I may say so,' he cried. 'We are most grateful to you.'

Roth cowered back into his hiding place, pointing to the metal fragment in the Doctor's other hand. 'Scavenger,' he breathed, staring wildly at it.

'Scavenger . . .' the Doctor repeated, recalling something Vural had said to him during his interrogation at the cave.

'Alien ... Alien ...' Roth jabbered, nodding and pointing.

'He's afraid of everything,' Sarah murmured, 'even his old crewmates.'

The Doctor stared down at the metal fragment. 'I don't blame him for being wary of friend Vural,' he said quietly.

Sarah shivered, and gazed anxiously around them. 'Doctor, what do think this ... this Alien can be?' she murmured. For a moment the Doctor said nothing. Then he stuffed the piece of Terullian into one of his many pockets, and stood quite still, as if in a trance.

All at once he roused himself and gestured irritably towards the pit. 'It's just typical of Harry,' he cried, without answering Sarah's question. 'How could anyone fall down a gaping subsidence like that ...' The Doctor paused and clutched his hat more firmly about his disordered curls. 'Of course,' he cried. 'Subsidence ... an old sewer perhaps ... or even the Piccadilly Line.'

'You mean there might be a way out at the bottom?' Sarah asked hopefully, trying to follow the Doctor's train of thought.

'There usually is,' the Doctor replied, quickly testing the knot which secured the two halves of his scarf together, and then making several turns with one of the free ends around a stunted pillar of rock beside the hole. He thrust the shorter end into Roth's trembling hands and motioned Sarah to take hold as well. Before she could protest, he had flung the longer end of the scarf into the pit and was preparing to climb down.

'Hang on,' he cried, 'I shan't be long.'

Sarah looked at him in horror. 'Doctor,' she shouted, 'if you fall, we'll never get you out.'

The Doctor gave a swashbuckling wave of his hat. 'I'm sure you won't let me down,' he cried, and slid abruptly out of sight.

Sarah watched the thick, woollen stitching stretch into a taut, narrow rope as it took the Doctor's considerable weight. The turns about the spike of rock held, and Roth and Sarah felt the vibrations of the scarf as the Doctor lowered himself down, hand over hand.

'I hope it's long enough,' Sarah murmured. She turned to Roth. His swarthy face had gone deathly pale. Suddenly he began to gibber, his whole body shaking.

'Na ... na ... na ...' he muttered.

Then Sarah heard it: the undulating hum of the Scavenger approaching over the boulders behind them. She clung tightly to the vibrating scarf. 'Doctor,' she screamed, 'it's here ... it's here ...' There was a sudden hissing through the air and a segmented strand of wire lashed itself around her wrist, gripping it so fiercely that in a few seconds her hand was completely numbed. With another whiplike sound, Roth was similarly caught. The scarf slipped from their grasp and started to unwind from its anchorage around the stump. There came a muffled cry from the pit and the scarf went slack.

42

Sick with fright, Sarah glanced round. The robot was hovering a few metres away, at the head of the ravine, its baleful, electronic eye fixed on her and Roth. It swivelled its scanner and all but wrenched them off their feet as it rose and began to glide away out of the ravine, drawing the defenceless humans screaming and stumbling in its wake.

The Doctor lay among the tangled reeds and boulders, the end of the scarf loose in his limp hands. Blood welled up from a deep gash in his ashen forehead. The breath gurgled in his throat, and he lay utterly still.

Harry felt his way along a tortuously narrow fissure which led first upwards and then downwards; to the right and then to the left, and which sometimes twisted round and round in a spiral. The heat was rapidly becoming unbearable, and he could scarcely touch the sides of the shaft. The strange rhythmic pulses surging through the rocky labyrinth were beating in his head like a monstrous drum, and the suffocating fumes grew thicker at every step.

As he stumbled through the choking fog, Harry felt the tunnel begin to open out. The drumming gradually reached a climax, and he suddenly found himself in a kind of chamber which was dimly lit by a natural phosphorescence of the rock walls and roof. In the centre of the chamber floor, huge, murky bubbles were forming in a pool of hot, viscous mud and bursting in clouds of dense gas whose detonations echoed around the network of tunnels.

Clasping his handkerchief tightly over his nose and mouth, Harry began to skirt round the sides of the molten cauldron, seeking a way out of the chamber. Suddenly he stopped dead in his tracks, pressing himself back as close as he dared to the scorching rock, and straining to see through the acrid gloom.

Something was splashing heavily about in the middle of the bubbling lava. The hair prickled on Harry's neck as he detected a slow, ponderous breathing sound above the noise of the exploding bubbles. He could see nothing. His head was reeling with the intense heat, and for a moment Harry feared he might collapse into the boiling mud. The splashing stopped. His heart hammering against his ribs, Harry listened to the monstrous, laboured breathing only a few metres away from him. He fought desperately against the choking cough trying to rise in his throat.

Suddenly, the ground shook under his feet as something began to move away with a stamping tread. The breathing grew fainter and fainter ... Banishing his fear in his panic to escape from the scorching underground maze, Harry edged his way as quietly as he could round the chamber. He soon came upon a large aperture—big enough for him to enter upright—in which the air seemed slightly clearer and cooler. With frequent pasuses to check for the slightest movement in the darkness, Harry crept cautiously along the tunnel. Its twists and turns soon revealed a circular patch of light ahead.

Eagerly he hurried forward, and was about to

break into a run when something appeared to step out of the tunnel wall just in front of him. He went rigid. The distant patch of daylight was momentarily blotted out by an obscure, massive shape which began to move ponderously away along the tunnel. Harry watched in horrified fascination as the heavy footsteps pounded along accompanied by stentorian breathing.

As the sounds receded, an enormous figure—like the statue of a huge, thick-limbed man somehow brought to life—was gradually silhouetted against the circle of daylight. As it lumbered out of the far end of the tunnel into the open, Harry glimpsed its coarse greyish hide—like pumice stone—shuddering at each step. He began to shiver in a sudden cold sweat.

'It ... it can't be ...' he gasped, as the gigantic figure stamped away into the distance, '... it isn't possible ... but it looks like the Golem ...'

For several minutes Harry stood motionless in the dark tunnel, staring at the gradually diminishing form of the monstrous creature. His imagination conjured up visions of a ruined world populated by colossal human mutations produced as a result of the Solar Flares which, the Doctor had explained, had rendered the Earth uninhabitable by normal animal and vegetable life.

Gradually he pulled himself together and cautiously edged forward towards the mouth of the tunnel. He was desperately anxious to escape from the labyrinth of subterranean shafts and chambers, and yet he was filled with foreboding as to what might await him in the open terrain. Keeping at a safe distance, he followed the tunnel towards daylight ...

The Scavenger dragged its two victims brutally through rocky gullies filled with great clusters of giant thorns which tore at their clothes and threatened to lacerate their faces. Deposits of orange dust rose in choking clouds and sucked them down like quicksand. Whenever Sarah or Roth hesitated or stumbled, the robot would pause, rotate its scanner towards them, chattering angrily to itself, and then viciously jerk the culprit to his feet with a twitch of its gleaming tentacle. In one place, where the thorns were several metres deep, the machine had simply blasted a pathway through them with a dazzling spray of white fire from its sensors.

'We're obviously wanted in reasonable condition ...' Sarah had muttered to herself, sickened by the oily, black smoke billowing from the molten undergrowth.

With her free hand, she frequently clutched at the withered and numbed object hanging limply from her other wrist—caught in the robot's relentless grasp. Her face was streaked with tears, dust and dried blood.

Beside her, Roth flapped along as if in a trance, whimpering his ceaseless refrain, 'Na ... na ... na ...' until, after what seemed hours, the Scavenger suddenly slowed and they entered a shallow, bowl-shaped area in the centre of a vast crater. Deep 'V' shaped canyons radiated from the rock-strewn hollow in all directions, leading to the encircling range of cliffs. Roth immediately pitched forward to his knees, staring and gesticulating towards a massive spherical object dominating the middle of the hollow. The Scavenger stopped and lowered itself so that it hovered a few centimetres above the ground. Then, after emitting a series of extremely high-pitched bleeps, it fell silent.

Sarah stared at the enormous dimpled sphere in front of them. It was the size of a large house and resembled a giant golf-ball. The red sun was brilliantly reflected from its metallic surfaces as if it were encrusted with rubies. Roth was now silent, mesmerised by the extraordinary globe. The Scavenger's tentacle had slackened a little and Sarah massaged her wrist and waited with thumping heart, her eyes fixed on an oval opening in the lower side of the sphere from which a ramp led down to the ground.

After a while, the Scavenger's relays clattered and it stirred slightly. In a flash, Sarah forgot the agonising pins-and-needles sensation in her hand and the pains throbbing in her bruised and exhausted body: from the dark opening in the huge sphere came a strangely familiar, but not at once recognisable, sound. It was the laboured breathing of some vast nightmarish bellows, and it sent icy shudders through Sarah's limbs.

All at once, the gaping oval panel was filled by a squat, lumbering shape like a monstrous puppet. Its domed, reptilian head grew neckless out of massive, hunched shoulders. Each trunk-like arm ended in

47

three sheathed talons and was raised in anticipation towards her. The creature began to lurch down the ramp on thick, stumpy legs, the rubbery folds of its body vibrating with each step. Mean eyes burned like two red-hot coals amid the gnarled, tortoise-like features, and puffs of oily vapour issued from the flared nostrils. As it approached her, the creature uttered a raucous gasp of satisfaction, 'Aaaaaaaaaaaa ... The female of the species ...'

The blubbery, gasping voice sent a tingle of recognition through Sarah. 'Linx ...' she murmured in disbelief, flinching away in disgust at the warm, sickly breath as the creature stood over her. The wobbling folds of its lipless jaws were suddenly drawn back, baring hooked, metallic teeth. Sarah stared transfixed at the ghastly smile while the creature slowly shook its domed head.

'But ... but Linx is dead ...' she managed to blurt. 'You were destroyed ... in the Thirteenth Century ...'

The creature continued to shake its head. 'You may have witnessed the demise of one of our number,' it gasped, 'but we are many.' The shrivelled, tortoise face thrust forward, its red piercing eyes boring into her. 'I am Styr ... Sontaran Military Assessor.'

Sarah forced herself to stare defiantly back. 'And what are you assessing?' she found herself retorting with a contemptuous toss of her head.

There was a menacing pause and then the creature seized Sarah's arm in its leathery claw. 'I shall continue,' gasped the wobbling mouth, 'with *you*.'

At that moment Roth, who had been cowering

48

silently at Sarah's side, sprang up, taking advantage of the loosening of the Scavenger's tentacle. 'Not me ...' he shrieked, breaking into a run. 'Na ... na ... you won't hurt me again ...' and he made off towards one of the nearby ravines. Styr raised his arm and aimed a small device like a wristwatch, which was incorporated into his sleeve. The fleeing crewman was enveloped in an intense white light and crashed lifeless onto the rocks.

Sarah found that anger and contempt were beginning to conquer her fear. 'That was senseless,' she cried. 'He was harmless.'

The Sontaran turned on her with a snort of oily vapour. 'And quite useless,' he gasped, gripping her arm even more fiercely. 'He was of no further significance to my programme.' Sarah tried to wrench herself free, averting her face from the Sontaran's nauseating breath, but he lifted her roughly against his pulsing, rubbery abdomen.

'Whereas you,' Styr hissed, 'you are of much greater value for my purposes.'

Styr drew a small spherical microphone, attached to a retractable cable, from a battery of strange instruments arrayed round his belt, and without relinquishing his cruel grip on Sarah's arm, began to gasp excitedly into it, 'Assessment Period Gamma ... Solar Interval Eleven ... Human Female—First Specimen ...' His sparkling eyes glittered centimetres from Sarah's face. '... No apparent strategic significance ... presence on Earth Planet unexplained ... result of tests will follow ...' The microphone snapped

49

back into its housing and the Sontaran tapped out rapid instructions on the touch-button panel in the front of his belt.

At once the Scavenger clattered its relays in acknowledgement. It retracted its tentacles, rose a metre into the air and glided out of the hollow into one of the ravines, its scanner sweeping from side to side as it hummed out of sight.

'Soon I shall have your companions,' hissed Styr, dragging Sarah along as he lumbered towards one of the gullies on the far side of the hollow, 'but for the present ... we shall proceed with *you* ...'

The Doctor moaned and stirred slightly. Then he began to thrash about in spasms of panic. The TARDIS was surrounded by a host of colossal rats, their teeth squeaking against the frosted glass windowpanes and their claws tearing at the creaking woodwork of the battered police box. The wretched machine was completely out of control, and nothing the Doctor could do would make it respond. It had drifted too close to the edge of a rotating black hole and been pitched and tossed like a cork in a typhoon, hurling the Doctor against the controls. His head raging with pain, he struggled to activate the stabilisers as the voracious rats gnawed hungrily at the windows, fighting to get at him.

Just as they seemed to be on the point of breaking in, a huge black cat, its fur on end and its claws gleaming viciously, sprang out from the TARDIS's

Control Assembly, spitting and snarling, and devoured all the rats in an instant. Then, purring contentedly, it stretched out on the Doctor's chest and went to sleep. The Doctor lay on the floor of the TARDIS, struggling for breath beneath the heavy, furry body pressing against his face.

'Off ... Off Greymalkin ... Off ...' he panted, grabbing the warm fur in both hands and trying to fling the enormous creature aside ...

The Doctor came to in the semi-darkness. He was flat on his back among sharp rocks, his whole body aching. He was clutching his hat screwed up in both hands at arm's length above his face. He raised his head and blinked a few times, wincing with pain. After a minute or two he shook himself.

'Rats ...' he muttered scornfully and dragged himself slowly to his feet, rubbing his eyes and peering around. He pushed his hat back into shape and set it gingerly on top of his throbbing head.

There was a sudden rustling and scrambling sound above him. For a second the Doctor hesitated, not quite sure whether he was still dreaming, or whether he really was awake. He looked up at the daylight. The pit seemed even deeper from where he stood now.

'Sarah ... Sarah Jane?' he called softly. The sounds abruptly ceased. Something brushed the Doctor's face: it was the scarf. He tested the swaying, woollen ladder. To his intense relief it held.

'Sarah ... I'm coming back up,' he cried. Still there was no reply. The Doctor shrugged and began to pull himself slowly and painfully upwards.

When at last his head appeared above the edge of the hole, he saw a blurred, triple image of Roth watching him from the cluster of boulders.

'Hallo,' he cried, blinking furiously, 'I really must have banged my head down there. Where's Sar ...' The Doctor's cheery voice died away: the space-suited figures of Vural, Krans and Erak stood watching him with ironic smiles. Vural was gripping the end of the scarf securely round its anchorage, while Erak held an ion gun levelled straight at the Doctor's head. Sarah and Roth were nowhere to be seen.

The Doctor grinned faintly. 'Oh ... it's you again,' he murmured.

'Keep climbing,' Vural snapped. 'And no tricks.'

The Doctor shook his head. 'Absolutely no tricks,' he agreed, his eyes flickering up for a second to something which had suddenly appeared above and behind his three captors. 'Not *this* deal anyway,' he added, starting to heave himself up on his elbows. Krans started forward threateningly, a machete gleaming in his hand. At the same moment, the Scavenger whirred into the air above the boulders. Before the three crewmen could react, its tentacles had whipped through the thin mist and snared each of them simultaneously.

With a choking cry, Krans flung up his hands and tugged helplessly at the loop around his neck, the ion gun flew out of Erak's numbed grasp, and Vural, both arms pinioned tightly to his body, tried to back away, shaking his head in panic and muttering, 'Not me ... no ... the others ... but not me ...' while the electronic scanner fixed him with its expressionless stare.

'Trumps!' cried the Doctor, and with a victorious wave, he slid swiftly back into the protective gloom of the pit ...

4

The Experiment

After his narrow escape in the subterranean labyrinth, Harry had stalked the monstrous figure of the 'Golem' through the rocky wilderness. From a vantage point high on one of the ridges radiating across the crater, he had witnessed Sarah's terrifying encounter with the creature in front of its hidden lair. He knew he had no chance of rescuing Sarah single-handed; his only hope was to discover where Sarah was being taken, and then to try and find the Doctor.

As he scrambled through the maze of canyons and intersecting gullies criss-crossing the crater in pursuit of Sarah and her hideous captor, Harry racked his brain to remember the story of the Golem—the manmade effigy brought to life by means of the Shem, the magic charm, destruction of which would render the creature lifeless again ... But it was all too fantastic, he told himself as he dodged between pinnacles and buttresses of rock, in a landscape which suggested the petrified remains of a medieval city, melted and deformed by some catastrophe. The similarity sent a shiver through him, and he quickened his pace, anxious not to lose sight of his quarry.

The wind moaned through the twisted rocks and

echoed around him like the cries of ghostly victims or unknown and unimaginable beings. He felt sure that at any moment the luminous hovering shape of the robot would come gliding suddenly out of some concealed niche, or that a host of gasping, lumbering creatures would trap him in one of the defiles which branched in all directions.

All at once Harry stopped, biting his lip in frustration. Sarah and the Golem had vanished. He had lost them. He glanced up at the glowering sun, trying to orientate himself. The whining breezes mocked him. It was hopeless. Then, from a nearby cleft in the rock, there came a chilling cry of agony. Arming himself with a small boulder, Harry approached.

'Sarah ... Sarah, is that you ... ?' he called softly. A feeble, cracked voice tried to answer. Cautiously Harry squeezed in among the thorns.

A young man, emaciated and deathly pale, with long matted hair and beard, was manacled to the rock by his wrists so that his arms were fully stretched above his head and his feet scarcely touched the ground. The ripped-open top of his space-suit hung in ribbons round his waist, and Harry winced at the sight of the wasted torso with sharply protruding ribs.

'Who did this?' he breathed, tugging vainly at the strange metallic shackles which seemed to be welded into the rock.

'Wa ... water ... wa ...' the prisoner gasped through cracked and blackened lips, his head lolling from side to side.

Harry thrust the stone he was carrying under the

victim's feet to help support his weight. 'All right, old chap,' he murmured. 'I'll soon get you some water.'

Harry searched feverishly among the rocks, but he knew it was quite pointless. Everything was scorched and bone dry. He had seen no pools or streams anywhere. He ran back to the dying man, and listened intently to the spasmodic fluttering of his failing heart.

'Did the ... the Golem thing do this to you?' he asked.

The young man tried to shake his head, staring at Harry with glazed, bloodshot eyes. 'Not ... not Golem ...' he croaked with a shudder, 'Son ... Sontaran ...'

Harry frowned, trying hard to understand the prisoner's cryptic utterances. 'Sontaran?' he echoed. The word meant nothing to him.

The young crewman nodded feebly and began to murmur between desperate snatches of breath, 'Sontaran ... in the hollow ... Experiments with the others ... others dead ... Scavenger comes ... at night ... we were helpless ...'

Harry clenched his fists in fury at the plight of the dying youth.

'Virtually dehydrated, poor chap,' he muttered. He knew full well that despite all his medical expertise, there was nothing he could do. The young crewman would not last another hour. 'I'm going to get help,' he murmured gently. 'You're going to be just fine ...' Reluctantly, he turned away.

Dry-mouthed, and with a funny feeling in his

stomach, Harry struck out through the maze of out-crops and gullies to try and locate the circle of spheres and, hopefully, to find the Doctor. He hardly dared imagine what Sarah's fate would be if he failed.

The Sontaran had dragged Sarah into a roofless alcove almost completely concealed between sheer rock buttresses which formed a narrow entrance less than a metre wide. The smooth, sheer walls towering into the sky were veined with filaments of coloured strata, and the floor of the alcove was carpeted with what looked like brilliant mosses. Despite her apprehension, Sarah could not suppress a gasp of wonder at the unexpected beauty of the place.

Styr loomed in the entrance, barring any escape. 'Lying is useless,' he threatened. 'When I waylaid the Galsec craft there were nine survivors: you were not among them.'

Sarah stood in the centre of the chamber, massaging her bruised wrist. 'So?' she challenged, her jaw jutting defiantly forward.

'I ask you once more,' Styr rasped. 'What is your planet of origin?'

'I've told you—Earth,' Sarah repeated.

Styr raised his thick, powerful arms and clenched his enormous talons. 'There has been no intelligent life on Earth since the time of the Solar Flares,' he roared.

'Oh, I'm much older than the Solar Flares,' Sarah sniffed with mock haughtiness.

Styr's hog-like nostrils expanded, ejecting a stream of clammy, rancid vapour. Amazed at her own courage, Sarah forced herself to face her monstrous captor without flinching.

'That is not possible,' Styr bellowed.

Sarah shrugged. 'There's no point in getting all steamed up about *me*,' she retorted. 'I'm really quite insignificant.' For a moment the Sontaran, powerful and menacing though he was, seemed disconcerted by Sarah's defiant manner. Then he suddenly lurched forward towards her, his eyes glowing red and hissing like two gas-jets.

'According to our data, you should not exist,' he gasped. 'Therefore we must investigate the implications of your presence here, and make the necessary corrections.'

Sarah imagined the huge rubbery lungs inflating and collapsing like vast bellows as the Alien's hollow gasps echoed round the alcove. 'Corrections to what?' she asked, standing her ground with hands on hips.

'To the project,' Styr breathed, towering over her.

Sarah fought against the feeling of nausea welling in her stomach. 'Project?' she inquired, determined to play for time, and to glean as much as she could before being subjected to whatever fate the Sontaran intended for her.

Styr swung heavily round and tramped towards the opening between the rocks. 'It will not concern you,' he rasped. 'You will not exist.' Raising a massive arm, Styr adjusted something set into one of the flanking buttresses. At once, a faint barrier like thick uneven glass appeared across the entrance to the alcove. Styr bared his curved, metallic teeth in a leathery, reptilian grin. 'But first,' he concluded, 'we shall discover what you are made of ...' Then he turned and lumbered away.

Sarah waited for a moment and then ran towards the opening. Even before she reached it she knew there was no escape. The narrow space between the buttresses wobbled like a distant heat haze, and the air surrounding it crackled as if with a fierce electric charge. She sank down disconsolately in the centre of the mossy floor, utterly alone. Harry had disappeared and the Doctor was lying injured—or perhaps even dead—at the bottom of the pit. There seemed to be no hope for her. She was completely at Styr's mercy.

As her hands ruffled the moss around her, she suddenly glanced down and then examined the multi-coloured 'carpet' more closely: it was not moss at all, but a vast cluster of tiny ends of wire. She sprang up and peered closely at the walls of the alcove: what appeared to be intermingling veins of different rock strata were in fact wire elements embedded in the rock surface. Just as she stretched out her hand to touch them, the whole alcove seemed to suddenly come alive around her.

With a thunderous tearing sound, the surrounding rock began to bulge and twist into nightmare shapes. Gigantic gnarled faces with bottomless pits for eyes, and grinning mouths bristling with razor-edged fangs, burst out at her from the heaving walls of the alcove. Bubbles of loathsome, oozing liquid seeped from thousands of tiny fissures and formed into strands of molten rock—thin as cobwebs—which enveloped her like a cocoon. It seemed to Sarah that unmentionable horrors which had lain hidden at the back of her mind all her life were suddenly becoming reality all around her.

She flung herself onto the undulating floor and covered her face and screamed as the rock reared up in waves and folded around her, engulfing her slowly like a huge, bellowing maw ...

The Doctor was eagerly exploring the depths of the pit using the sonic screwdriver—switched to photon emission mode—as a torch.

'Fascinating,' he muttered as the sharp beam illuminated a cluster of bubbles of rock swelling out of the cavern wall like huge boils. 'A sudden release of pressure in the magma ...' he mused, sweeping the beam over the glassy surfaces. 'The temperatures must have been colossal ...' He tapped one of the bubbles with his finger. 'Certainly not the Piccadilly Line,' he murmured, sniffing the warm sulphurous air. 'Smells more like the basement of the Savoy ... which reminds me,' he suddenly cried, 'I haven't had any breakfast ...'

The Doctor listened intently to the mingling echoes of his voice until they had died away. 'Sounds like the Whitehall warren,' he exclaimed, directing the sonar-photon beam into a gaping black opening above his head. Then stumbling across the mound of shattered rock, he seized the dangling end of the scarf.

'This is no time for idle speculation,' he told himself, giving the scarf a sharp tug. It immediately fell in a series of snakelike coils around him. For a moment, the Doctor stared at it with a mortified look and then glanced up at the edge of the pit, five or six metres above him.

'Harry couldn't have gone *that* way,' he muttered. He scrambled back and peered up into the dark shaft again. The sonic torch-beam revealed protruding spurs of rock studding the twisting sides of the shaft before it curved away into darkness. With a few quick movements, the Doctor deftly fashioned a small lassoo with one end of the scarf. He then flung it into the shaft several times, as high as he could. At last it hooked itself round one of the projecting spurs and the Doctor pulled the loop tight.

'Hope I don't burst in on a Cabinet Meeting,' he grinned, and hoisted himself rapidly into the booming honeycomb of tunnels.

Harry lay flattened amongst a dense mass of gigantic thorns, oblivious of their piercing sting as he strained his ears to locate the direction of the eerie humming. He had searched for what seemed like hours to find a way out of the crater, trying to use the massive red sun as a bearing, but in vain. Then the sinister throbbing of the robot had startled him and sent him diving into the nearest cover. He thought he also heard the hoarse cries of several men echoing through the gullies.

To his relief the sounds faded away after several

minutes and Harry emerged, tugging the poisonous-looking spines out of his hair and hands. He made his way along a broad ridge which looked familiar, scanning the terrain for some recognisable feature.

Suddenly the ground seemed to gape open and an ear-shattering scream exploded into the air in front of him. He found himself teetering on the brink of a deep crevasse between tall pillars of rock. Thirty metres below him lay Sarah Jane, her hands clutching her head, writhing in agony. For a moment Harry could not move. Then he half rolled, half fell down the steep slope of the ridge into the ravine, and searched frantically along the base of the range of buttresses until he found the narrow opening into the bottom of the crevasse.

As Harry ran through the slit, a gigantic fist sent him flying back into the ravine. He sprawled in the undergrowth, knocked almost senseless. When he managed to sit up, he saw Sarah crouching in the middle of the alcove, her hands tearing wildly at her hair and her eyes fixed upon some invisible horror at which she was screaming soundlessly, her whole face contorted.

Harry staggered towards her and was once again sent reeling and flailing like a broken puppet back into the reeds. His head spinning and his nose bleeding, he crept towards the opening a third time and sank to his knees, staring at Sarah through the shimmering, invisible barrier. He put out his hand cautiously. It met a wall of solid, vibrating air.

'Sarah . . . I can't reach you . . . I just can't get in . . .'

he called weakly. He watched helplessly as Sarah began to make panic-stricken movements as if she were fighting for breath. 'What on earth is that creature doing to you?' he gasped, wiping the blood from his nose and lips. Sarah had gone completely rigid, her face a frozen mask. Harry tottered to his feet.

'Don't you worry, old thing,' he cried. 'I'll get you out of there if it's the last thing I do. Just let me get my hands on that animated lump of rubber. He'll need more than his magic words and charms before I'm through with him ...'

But Sarah did not hear Harry's desperate threats as he stumbled away into the rocks in search of her tormentor. She fought to stay afloat in the raging sea which suddenly burst around her. The waves threw her spreadeagled into the icy wind, and then dropped her like a stone into freezing green chasms which closed over her. Stinging fingers of salt water and her own, gale-whipped hair lashed and blinded her. The wind tore the breath out of her lungs and drove it shrieking through her head. Vast, unnameable creatures thrashed in the depths around her, threatening to crush her between their dark flanks as she sank and sank ...

Just as she was on the point of losing consciousness, the wild movements abruptly ceased. Sarah found herself lying motionless on a vast plain of scorching sand, her whole body paralysed. She felt her skin splitting and crackling in the ferocious heat, curling layers of it peeling away from her like the skins of an onion.

When she tried to cry out, her parched throat uttered a series of rasping croaks which rang in the emptiness around her. The gigantic disc of the sun swelled until it filled the entire sky. She felt her eyes shrivelling in their sockets, and as she gasped for air her lungs filled with molten lead which rapidly solidified, transforming her into a mummified metal figure, lying rigid in the endless desert ...

Styr gloated over Sarah's suffering with cold, contemptuous amusement as he adjusted the array of instruments massed around the circular Survey Control Module, buried deep in the heart of the enormous, spherical Sontaran spacecraft.

'Such puny creatures ...' he breathed, his eyes glinting in fascination as Sarah's terror-stricken features zoomed into closeup on the shimmering monitor panel. At the back of his partly organic, partly mechanical mind there lurked serious doubts about the origin of this female human and her associates. They did not fit into the picture of Earth as a sterile, abandoned planet, the theory which the Sontaran Strategic Council had sent him to confirm.

However, Styr's sadistic delight in torture seemed to have blinded him to the true purpose of his Assessment Expedition. He stared at Sarah's exhausted, motionless face.

'A brief respite ...' he gasped, his talons twitching with impatience. 'We must not destroy such an interesting specimen too quickly.'

At that moment, Sarah's body began to quiver in rapid feverish spasms, her hands making frantic brushing movements in the air. Styr punched several switches on his console and peered more closely.

'Aaaaaaaaagh,' he nodded, his eyes glowing in anticipation. 'The Formicidae ...' He watched the monitor panel intently, making constant adjustments to the instruments surrounding it. Sarah was staring at the ground in panic and shuddering convulsively. Styr's wheezing breath quickened and he uttered a rattling gurgle of delight. 'Strange to be so affected by such minute creatures,' he muttered, slowly turning a calibrated disc a full quarter circle with his clumsy, three-pincered hand. 'Let us see what happens if we make them rather larger ...' and he leaned eagerly towards the monitor panel so that its fluorescence played a menacing greenish aura over his wobbling features.

An urgent bleeping signal suddenly sounded from a small device clamped to Styr's belt. Hissing with frustration and rage, he snatched the communicator from its holder. 'Earth Survey,' he snapped, his eyes still fixed on Sarah's struggling form. On the communicator's display there appeared the squat, domed head of a Sontaran identical to Styr himself.

'We await your assessment, Styr,' the image rapped. 'Proceed at once.'

Reluctantly Styr tore his gaze from the monitor. Then his massive bulk began to swell with self-importance as he spoke into the portable receiver.

'The prediction is correct, Controller,' he announced. 'The Earth Planet has not been repopulated.

In accordance with the Strategic Council's instructions, I have lured a group of Humans from Galsec Colony to the Planet for investigation ...' Styr's eyes strayed furtively across to Sarah's contorted body glowing on the monitor panel ... 'and as predicted, they are puny beings with negligible resistance to physical or mental stress, and total dependence upon organic substances for survival ...'

'Excellent, excellent,' the Sontaran Controller interrupted impatiently. 'We shall proceed with the project immediately.'

The ghastly folds of Styr's face quivered with indignation. 'But my assessment is not yet complete,' he protested.

The Sontaran Controller glared angrily from the communicator display. 'Our information is sufficient; further delay is not necessary,' he announced. 'The Squadrons are primed and are preparing their formations for attack.'

Again Styr glanced covertly at Sarah's image: she was clawing desperately at some invisible horror in her gaping mouth. His vast body shook with a thrill of pleasure.

'I must have more time, Controller,' he blustered, his flapping jaws moist with blackish oily droplets.

'You will return to your Unit at once, Styr,' the Controller commanded, bursting with anger.

'An inconsistency has been detected,' Styr blurted, with a cunning pause. 'Certain data have just appeared which do not agree with our prediction.'

The Controller stared impassively. 'Explain,' he

ordered sharply.

'I have initiated a series of tests to determine the origin of certain unforeseen elements—beings whose presence on this planet is not yet explained,' Styr gasped, a devious gleam burning in his eyes. 'I must fulfill my responsibility to the Strategic Council.'

The Controller considered for a moment, a trace of suspicion in his glowering face. 'Then proceed, Styr, but quickly,' he snapped at last. 'Further delay could be catastrophic—and you know what the consequences would be to yourself . . .'

With that grim warning the communicator went dead. The Controller's relentless stare remained on the display for a few seconds, his eyes two lingering points of intense brightness. Then it faded. Styr remained motionless for some time, his scimitar-like teeth bared, and drops of oily saliva trickling from the corners of his grinning mouth onto his huge chest. Then, with eager, brutal jabs, he re-activated his instruments.

'You will be more useful than I realised,' he panted, his eyes beginning to hiss as he peered closely at the image of Sarah's crumpled body on the monitor. He gave the controls a vicious twist with both of his grasping clammy pincers, and his hunched bulky frame tensed in expectation . . .

5

Mistaken Identities

Sarah felt the white-hot sand begin to move beneath her. The grains prickled against her skin like millions of needles as they jostled and clustered. Weakened though she was, she tried to brush them away, but the more she struggled, the thicker they swarmed over her body. The whole desert was alive around her. She dragged herself to her feet, clawing blindly at the masses of stinging grains which covered her in a steadily growing layer. Her shrivelled eyes seemed to be prised out of their sockets and the burning particles began to force themselves up into her brain. She tried to cry out and was choked by a stream of sand which welled up from her blazing stomach.

With a stunning flash of light like an explosion, she found she could see again. The floor of the crevasse was crawling with enormous ants advancing in a seething mass from all sides. The air was filled with the rustle of their antennae as they fought to get at her, a helpless victim trapped at the centre of the nest. Even as she watched, transfixed, the creatures began to grow larger. Her whole body bristled with the ravenous insects and, quickly stripped of all its flesh, it soon became a fantastic buzzing skeleton which splintered and finally collapsed under the monstrous throng.

Harry stood poised on a narrow ledge above a cutting between two enormous outcrops of rock, pressing himself back as far as he could into a shallow niche behind him. With both hands he gripped a heavy stone, the shape and size of a rugger ball, and strained his ears to judge the approach of the slow, ponderous footsteps which were coming along the gully towards him.

Suddenly the footsteps stopped. Harry stood on the tips of his toes, raising the stone as high as he could above his head. He held his breath, waiting for the slightest movement. Something flashed into view round the edge of the niche and Harry pitched forward, hurling the stone downwards with all his strength. He crashed face-down on top of the boulder and froze as a deafening bellow ripped through the air behind him. He lay quite still, the breath knocked out of him, waiting to be trampled or torn to pieces by the enraged Alien.

'Not a bad try, Harry,' boomed a familiar voice. Harry rolled over on to his back and gasped with relief as he saw the Doctor looking down at him with a grin. 'But I shouldn't try to convert it if I were you,' the Doctor added, heaving the murderous missile off the squashed remains of his hat and shoving the crown back into shape.

Harry shook his head ruefully. 'Sorry about that,

Doctor ... I th ... thought you were the ... the Humpty Dumpty thing,' he stammered breathlessly.

'Humpty Dumpty?' the Doctor echoed, cramming the hat so firmly back on his head that the crown was pushed up into a dome and his ears were bent over by the brim. For a moment Harry just lay there, struck dumb by an uncanny resemblance, and all he could manage was a series of frantic nods.

'The Sont ... Sontaran ...' he cried at last.

The Doctor's eyes widened. He leaned down and helped Harry to his feet. 'Sontaran?' he murmured. 'Here?'

Harry nodded again, desperately trying to remember what the dying prisoner had said. 'Thing like ... like some kind of Golem ...' he frowned.

The Doctor took Harry's arm and began to walk quickly along the gully. 'The Sontarans are all identical clone-creatures,' he explained, 'composed of complex hypercatalysed polymers in conjunction with molecular ...'

'Complex *whats?*' Harry gasped. The Doctor threw him a reproachful glance. 'Sorry, Doctor,' he muttered. 'Afraid my chemistry didn't get that far ...'

The Doctor resumed his explanation, waving his arms in the air and speaking so rapidly that Harry soon gave up trying to understand him. As he strode along, the Doctor held forth for several minutes, so absorbed in his subject that he was quite oblivious of Harry's attempts to interrupt.

'... and so their brains are rather like seaweed and their lungs are made from a kind of spongy steel-wool,' he at last concluded, suddenly stopping to look

70

up at the sky.

'But where do they *come* from?' asked Harry.

'No one quite knows,' the Doctor replied, taking from one of his pockets the piece of Terullian he had picked up at the edge of the pit, and gently rubbing it with his thumb. 'They have not been reported in this galaxy since the Middle Ages.' Suddenly, the small metallic fragment began to vibrate with a sound like that made by a glass tumbler when its rim is stroked with a moistened finger.

'I wonder what mischief they can be up to now, Harry,' the Doctor murmured, glancing round at the barren landscape.

Harry had been mesmerised by the eerie, ringing sound coming from the Doctor's hand. Suddenly he pulled himself together. 'One of them has got Sarah trapped in some kind of ...'

The Doctor swung round on him sharply. 'Sarah Jane ... ?' he cried. 'Why didn't you say so before?' Harry shrugged in confusion. The Doctor thrust the Terullian fragment into his pocket and gathered up his scarf-ends. 'Where is she?' he demanded.

Just as Harry opened his mouth to reply, an unearthly, piercing shriek rang out and echoed through the ravines.

'Sarah!' the Doctor gasped. Instantly he started off up the side of the ravine, slipping and sliding as he disappeared over the top of the ridge.

'Doctor, she's trapped: you can't reach her,' Harry called, but the Doctor had gone. Wearily, Harry set off in pursuit.

The Doctor stared in dismay through the impenetrable barrier stretched between the rocky buttresses. 'My poor Sarah Jane,' he murmured. 'Whatever have they done to you ...'

Sarah's body lay motionless in the centre of the alcove, her limbs contorted and rigid, her face streaked with tears and dust, and her eyes wide open but unseeing, without a flicker of life. The Doctor soon located the two small discs of Terullian mounted one on each side of the narrow entrance to Sarah's prison. He began to pace furiously up and down.

'A fluctuating geon field!' he cried, pounding the invisible barrier with his fist as he passed. 'I had no idea that Sontaran technology had progressed so far.'

Flushed with anger, he stopped and peered in at the inert figure of his young friend. 'A great pity that their morals have not kept pace with their science,' he muttered. He drew the battered ear-trumpet from his pocket and held it against one of the buttresses. As he listened, his brow furrowed with concentration, he began to solve a dazzling series of equations in his head. Eventually, he stuffed the ear-trumpet away and using the coloured divisions of his scarf, measured the distance between the two Terullian discs, taking great care not to touch them.

His face hardened with resolution, the Doctor stared at the two discs flanking the opening. 'There's no other way,' he murmured. 'I'll just have to increase the feedback and hope that the field gives way before I do ...' Taking a few deep breaths, the Doctor stretched out both arms and approached the barrier, bringing his hands closer and closer to the discs.

He fixed his eyes upon Sarah and tried to clear everything from his mind in preparation for the ordeal ahead. As his palms came nearer and nearer to the discs, his body began to tremble with the energy surging through them.

At last they touched. The Doctor roared with pain as stunning bolts of shock drove through his arms. His body was whipped back and forth like a sheet flapping in a gale. He fought to keep his mind clear, knowing that he must be able to judge the exact instant to break through the barrier before he was disintegrated. As he pressed his head against the wobbling, invisible wall, he felt the geon field weaken slightly, but the pulsing hammer-blows, racking his whole body, threatened to overwhelm him before the moment to penetrate the barrier was reached.

His hands were glued to the red-hot terminals and he felt as if his brain were being shaken rapidly to a jelly. At any moment he could be torn apart like a piece of rag. The Doctor strained desperately against the reduced geon field. Gradually it yielded until it had almost disappeared, but he could not free his hands from the searing metal discs. He seemed to be hopelessly trapped...

The Scavenger hovered patiently in front of the Sontaran space-craft in the hollow landing area. Vural, Krans and Erak sank to their knees, exhausted by the terrible ordeal of being dragged across the rough terrain, tethered to the merciless machine. Since their capture, Vural had been strangely silent. Krans and Erak kept their eyes fixed on the open hatch in the side of the huge dimpled sphere, dreading to think what fate was in store for them.

'You'll see ...' growled Krans, nodding towards the gleaming space-craft, '...that crazy joker will turn up again with more of his tricks. We shoulda finished him when we had the chance.'

'If you two hadn't been so keen to chase after Roth, we wouldn't be in this mess,' Erak retorted.

The dispute died on their lips as the huge figure of Styr suddenly filled the open hatch.

'The Scout Unit would have found you in the end,' Styr hissed, his nostrils flaring as he stumped down the ramp towards them. 'Meanwhile, it has been most valuable to observe your curious behaviour patterns...' he gasped as he loomed over the three kneeling crewmen. Vural began to tremble violently as he cowered between Krans and Erak.

'Not me ... not ... not me ...' he gibbered, raising his numbed white hands in supplication.

'All of you,' Styr hissed, reaching down and tearing the miniature scanning device from round the Galsec Crew Leader's neck.

'But I helped you,' Vural whimpered. 'I did everything you wanted.'

'You failed to produce the unknown stranger from the circle,' Styr rasped. 'You lost him.'

Vural tried to shuffle forward on his knees, as if to attack the towering figure of the Sontaran with his helplessly pinioned arms. Styr thrust him back with a contemptuous kick.

74

'You promised ... you promised to spare me ...'
Vural went on.

Styr's squat features squeezed into a ghastly, ironic
smile. 'A simple test of human gullibility,' he gasped.
'Why should you be spared—a traitor to your own
miserable species?'

Krans and Erak stared incredulously at one another
as their leader's treachery was revealed. Krans
clenched his big fists. 'Lousy swine,' he spat. 'So you
tried to fix yourself a deal with this thing.'

Vural flinched away from Krans who was straining
to get at him, despite the Scavenger's tentacle wound
tightly round his neck. 'There was no other way,
Krans,' murmured Vural, his eyes fixed on Styr as if
hypnotised. 'It gave us more time ...'

'That first night—after the ship exploded—he was
missing for hours,' muttered Erak with narrowed
eyes.

'It was for *us*,' Vural shrieked, sweat pouring down
his face.

Styr, who had been observing the scene with scornful amusement, silenced the three crewmen with a
raucous hiss. He listened intently to the rapid series
of bleeps—like morse code—which had suddenly
issued from the communicator at his side. When the
transmission ceased, he hurriedly began tapping a
coded programme into the control unit built into his
belt. Chattering quietly, the Scavenger rose up and
tightened its grip on the three captives.

'You can resolve your pathetic dispute together in
the next experiment,' Styr gasped. 'I advise you to
conserve all your energies until then.'

75

With that, Styr turned abruptly away and lurched towards one of the ravines radiating from the hollow, his gimlet eyes blazing and his nostrils roaring with streams of vapour. The Scavenger glided smoothly towards an area covered with massive flat rocks on the other side of the landing area, the three crewmen stumbling painfully behind. It then began to prepare them for the most fiendish experiment of all.

The Doctor felt as if he had been falling for hours. Although he knew that his hands had only freed themselves from the Terullian discs a split-second previously, it seemed to be taking an eternity for him to thrust his way through the almost non-existent remains of the geon field. Suspended half way through the gap between the buttresses, he felt as though he were falling forward and yet not moving at all. The Doctor knew that without enough forward velocity he could be caught for ever, as long as the geon field persisted. There was absolutely nothing that even a Time Lord could do once he was caught up in it.

To his delight, he suddenly began to feel the slightest sensation of progress. Gradually at first, and then with increasing speed he felt himself toppling forward.

At last he staggered on to all fours inside the alcove where Sarah lay. For a few minutes he knelt there, fighting the nausea in his stomach and the agonising pains shooting through his whole body. Then he dragged himself across to Sarah.

'Sarah ... Sarah Jane?' he whispered, grasping her stiff, cold hands. There was no response. The Doctor glanced around at the walls of the crevasse, and then brushed at the ground with his blistered hands. Suddenly his eyes lit up with renewed hope. 'Neuro-Manipulation Chamber,' he breathed. Gently he shook Sarah by the shoulders. 'Sarah ... nothing has happened to you,' he murmured. 'Not really ... Do you understand me, my dear? It was all an illusion ... it was all in your mind.'

Something about Sarah's unblinking stare made the Doctor pause. He leaned forward and listened for her heartbeat. Then his face went white as marble. 'Oh, Sarah,' he murmured. 'Poor Sarah Jane ...'

'Very touching,' sneered a gasping voice behind him. The Doctor spun round to confront the pulsating figure of Styr in the entrance.

'You unspeakable abomination,' the Doctor murmured, rising slowly to his feet. 'Why have you done this?'

Styr snorted, his hoggish nostrils dilating and his curved teeth grinding shrilly against each other. 'I did nothing,' he retorted. 'I merely stimulated and revived the fears which lay buried in the female's subconscious. She was her own victim.'

'You senselessly destroyed an innocent girl,' the Doctor shouted. 'What possible harm could she have done to you and your kind?'

Styr ignored the accusation and lumbered forward several paces, his pincers opening and shutting impatiently. 'You would appear to have exceptional powers,' he panted, 'and will be a most interesting subject, much more worthy of investigation ...'

The Doctor sprang forward. Grabbing one arm, he swung it with all his strength and sent Styr's massively unwieldy frame trundling round and round like a run-down spinning top.

With a shattering roar of fury, Styr struggled to regain his balance, triggering the lethal weapon concealed in the sleeve of his suit as he lurched around. The Doctor frantically dodged the deadly bolts of radiation as they swept crazily round the alcove, blasting whole sections of the circuitry embedded in the rockface into flaring, molten fragments. Rapidly weakening, he dived underneath Styr's flailing arms and out into the ravine.

The Sontaran lumbered a few metres in pursuit, but the Doctor had disappeared. 'You will be found, wherever you are ...' Styr bellowed, and tramped back towards the crevasse where Sarah still lay among the smouldering circuits.

The Doctor ran blindly through the ravine, his lungs bursting and his two hearts swelling as if to choke him. The strength in his legs began to dissolve and he fell down a steep slope into a thick bed of brittle ferns, their stems shattering like machine gun fire into a cloud of fine blackish dust which hung in the air before settling in a thin layer over his crumpled body.

Harry moved cautiously through the rocks, calling out

in the eerie silence and all the time trying to banish from his mind the terrible images Sarah's agonised scream had created. The Doctor had far outstripped him, leaping through the gullies with the agility of a cat, and now he seemed to be completely lost again.

He soon came across the dead body of the young crewman, dangling from its manacles in the hidden cleft, the lolling tongue black and hideously swollen, the eyes turned up in their sockets.

'Murderer,' Harry muttered through teeth clenched in frustration and fury. He hurried on, even more apprehensive of what would await him when he found Sarah—assuming that he ever did find her.

As he battled his way through dense undergrowth, Harry suddenly caught sight of the Doctor's hat, snared on some huge thorns. He freed it and began to search around with mingled feelings of foreboding and relief. He soon found the Doctor's body hunched among the ferns, and listened anxiously to his chest for some sign of life. The Doctor's hearts were fluttering weakly, and his breathing was spasmodic and shallow. Harry quickly loosened the Doctor's scarf and jacket, rolled him on to his back, and began to apply artificial respiration.

After a time, he paused and listened for any signs of improvement; but the Doctor appeared to be steadily fading. 'Come on, Doctor ... Come on,' he gasped, pushing down on the Doctor's chest with strong, rhythmic presses. 'You've got an extra heart ... you ought to be able ... to do better than this.' Again Harry stopped and listened, shaking his head in despair. 'Please, Doctor ... Please ...' he entreated, resuming the treatment.

Harry carried on until he was exhausted, and was close to tears as he bowed his head in defeat, puzzled at the absence of any evident injury to the Doctor's body, apart from blistered palms.

'Fat lot of use I turned out to be as an M.O. on this expedition,' he muttered. Without drugs and equipment there seemed to be little more he could do. He could not save the Doctor.

Pulling himself together, he decided to continue his search for Sarah: at least he might be able to help *her*. As he turned reluctantly away, he heard something which made his blood run cold: the muffled, hollow gasping of the Sontaran. Instantly, Harry was fired with the desire for revenge. Losing all his fear, he ran along the ravine towards the sound. As he approached the opening to the crevasse, the Sontaran's breathy speech grew more intelligible.

'The reactions of the female subject remain unpredictable ...' Styr was saying, '... therefore the exact function of this organism cannot yet be evaluated ...'

Harry crept up and peered round the buttress. Styr was standing over Sarah's twisted body, dictating into his micro-recorder unit. Licking his lips, Harry eyed the Sontaran's colossal back and thick limbs. Then, very carefully, he armed himself with a large, knobbly flint from the foot of the buttress and waited, watching Styr's every move as the Sontaran began to examine the damaged circuits around the sides of the alcove.

'Further evaluation must be postponed while necessary adjustments are made,' Styr concluded into the micro-recorder as he completed his inspection.

Harry stepped into the entrance and aimed the flint at the back of Styr's head. Bending his body backwards like a bow, he flung the stone, but at the instant it left his hands it seemed to be snatched out of the air, and simultaneously his face was covered by something large and soft. He was pulled swiftly and silently backwards out of the crevasse and propelled along the ravine and into a crevice concealed in the undergrowth. For several seconds he was held struggling in a vice-like clasp.

'Ssssssssssssh,' hissed a voice into his ear. Harry stopped struggling, and his face was uncovered. The flint was thrust in front of his eyes. 'I'm quite ashamed of you, Harry,' whispered the Doctor's voice, 'attacking a chap from behind like that ...'

6

The Challenge

Harry gulped in amazement. 'Doctor ... I thought you were ...' he stammered.

'It wouldn't have worked, Harry,' the Doctor whispered, 'not unless you had hit him exactly in the right spot.' He gave Harry a sharp tap on the back of his neck. 'There. That's a Sontaran's Achilles Heel.'

'Thanks for the tip,' Harry murmured, still recovering from his fright. 'I'll try to remember that.'

The Doctor released Harry and began to rummage about in his overflowing pockets, muttering quietly away to himself.

'But I thought you were a goner,' Harry exclaimed, filled with shame at having abandoned the Doctor. 'I was quite sure there was nothing I ...'

The Doctor put his finger to his lips. 'I was merely relaxing, Harry,' he grinned. 'An old Tibetan trick at times of unusual stress: it helps to clear the mind.'

'Well, I must get you to teach me sometime,' Harry said, shaking his head in disbelief.

The Doctor was busily turning out an extraordinary assortment of objects into his upturned hat: marbles, pieces of twisted wire, shrivelled jelly babies, weird keys, a pirate's eye-patch, strange coins, sea shells, a dead beetle ... all manner of things were added to the swelling jumble.

'Now where, where did I put it?' the Doctor muttered irritably, delving into his bulging inside pockets and producing even more bizarre items of bric-a-brac.

'What are you looking for, Doctor?' Harry asked.

'My Liquid Crystal Instant Recall Diary,' the Doctor sighed. 'I'm sure that I made some useful notes about the Sontarans a few centuries ago ... It's absolutely vital that we find out what they are doing here on Earth.'

'Mostly torturing and killing innocent humans, as far as I can see,' Harry murmured gloomily.

The Doctor began stuffing the varied contents of his hat back into his many pockets. 'I really cannot be expected to keep everything in my head,' he complained, bending the ear-trumpet in half so it would take up less room. 'Never hoard unnecessary junk, Harry. It's fatal to clutter oneself up.'

Dipping into the hat Harry idly picked out the scrap of unfamiliar metal which he had seen the Doctor fiddling with earlier.

'What *is* this stuff?' he asked.

The Doctor glanced up from his laborious task. 'An alloy of Terullian,' he replied.

Harry looked blank. 'Terullian?' he queried.

'A very rare substance, much sought after by many of the civilisations in the Universe,' the Doctor explained. 'It has literally thousands of uses ... under certain conditions it can even behave like a living organism.'

Harry shuddered at the idea of a live metal. 'Where does it come from?' he murmured, hastily putting the fragment back in the pile of jumble.

'It is formed inside the crusts of planetary bodies by the action of stellar radiation,' the Doctor answered.

'By neutrinos and things ...' Harry suggested.

'Exactly, Harry,' the Doctor said warmly. 'But it is not found in this galaxy ...' The Doctor broke off, staring at Harry with piercing eyes. He snatched the scrap of Terullian out of the hat. 'Of course ...' he cried, 'the Solar Flares. It's just possible that the Sontarans are prospecting for Terullian here on Earth.'

Harry told the Doctor about his encounter with Styr in the subterranean cavern. The Doctor listened eagerly, nodding as the details began to fit into place in his mind.

'The Sontarans have made many enemies by monopolising the exploitation of Terullian deposits in several galaxies,' he murmured when Harry had finished. He put the fragment carefully away.

'A most useful clue, Harry,' the Doctor continued cheerfully. 'Never throw anything away ... you never know when such bits and pieces are going to come in handy.'

At that moment, Styr's heavy tread and laboured breath were heard nearby. The Doctor and Harry remained utterly still. Gradually the sounds died away as the Sontaran strode into the distance. The Doctor jammed on his emptied hat and darted out of the crevice, where he and Harry had been hiding, into the gully.

'I'm going to follow our cumbersome friend and see what else I can discover,' the Doctor whispered. 'Harry, you'd better do whatever you can for poor Sarah Jane,' and before Harry could reply, he had set off along the ravine, zig-zagging from crevice to crevice in pursuit of the Sontaran.

When Harry eventually located the crevasse where he had discovered Sarah, he approached the entrance extremely cautiously. To his surprise he found that he was able to enter quite easily: the invisible force-field had gone. He was even more surprised to find the alcove deserted: Sarah was nowhere to be seen.

'Humpty Dumpty must have taken her,' he muttered disconsolately, going over to search the deep shadows around the base of the towering granite walls. All of a sudden he felt very dizzy.

'What on earth . . . ?' he began, clutching his reeling head as he caught sight of the molten bunches of coloured filaments festooning the sides of the dungeon. Everything around him began to spin faster and faster and he flung himself backwards as something flew hissing and spitting out of the shadows like an angry wildcat. He rubbed his eyes and found himself staring down at the crouched figure of Sarah, a metre in front of him.

'It's . . . it's only me . . . old thing . . .' Harry stuttered, managing a faint smile of greeting. But the smile instantly faded and Harry went white as chalk. Sarah's teeth were bared like fangs, and her eyes were glaring crazily. She tensed her body as if preparing to spring at him.

Slowly Harry backed away, shaking his head in confusion. 'Sarah ... it's me ... Harry ...' he protested. Sarah's only response was to raise her arms threateningly. In each hand she wielded an ugly flint, roughly shaped like a blade with sharp serrated edges. Unearthly, guttural snarls issued from her foaming mouth as she began to edge towards him.

'Sarah ... you mustn't ... you're obviously not well after ... after your ...' Harry gasped, pressing himself against the rock as he tried to shake the dizziness out of his head. With a sudden shriek, Sarah pounced. Harry reeled aside just in time and staggered into the middle of the chamber.

Sarah was clinging to the twisted wires sprouting from the wall, her hair wildly tangled like a nest of snakes. Unable to move, Harry stared up at the grotesquely hissing spider-like creature poised above him.

'No ...' he screamed. '... No ...' and flung his arms up in protection as the creature sprang at him again. This time he did not escape. The loathsome thing clung to his shoulders, slashing at his face with its flint claws and driving them deep into his skull ...

The Doctor crouched among the weirdly sculpted rocks topping the ridge and studied the Sontaran space-craft glinting in the centre of the hollow.

'I wonder how many there are ... ?' he murmured, straightening out the crooked sections of his brass telescope and focusing the ancient instrument on the dark opening in the side of the huge, golf-ball structure. Then he scanned the surrounding area carefully. Styr was nowhere in sight.

Shutting the telescope with a resolute snap, he slowly emerged from his hiding place and advanced cautiously towards the space-craft, darting from boulder to boulder once he had left cover. He was just about to step on to the lower end of the inclined ramp which lead up to the hatchway, when he heard a familiar humming sound coming from the direction of some flattish, rectangular stones behind him. Stealthily, the Doctor reached into his pocket and drew out the Terullian fragment. Keeping as still as he could, he slowly raised his hand with the scrap of metal shielded in his palm.

A hazy image of the hovering robot was reflected in its semi-polished surface. The Doctor watched the Scavenger approach and stop five or six metres behind him.

'Beware of the dog,' the Doctor thought wryly. He began to rub his thumb gently round and round on the piece of Terullian so that it started to resonate with a steady, bell-like sound. The quiet clicking of the robot's circuits ceased abruptly, and it continued to hover in the air behind the Doctor, as if hypnotised by the penetrating vibrations.

Suddenly it began to chatter violently to itself. It

wobbled and shuddered and spun first one way, then the other. It lurched a metre or two closer to the Doctor's back, its greenish aura intensifying into a menacing glow. Gritting his teeth against the overwhelming resonance, the Doctor pressed harder and harder on the metal with his rotating thumb. He began to feel very faint, and his head rang as if it were trapped inside a gigantic tolling bell.

With his free hand, he managed to extract the sonic-screwdriver from among the clutter filling his pocket, and to prime the settings. Then, carefully angling his two hands, the Doctor directed the sonic beam so that it reflected off the scrap of Terullian, straight towards the threatening robot behind him. The sonic beam took over from the Doctor's burning thumb, causing the metal fragment to emit a highly focused stream of energy which no longer affected the Doctor, but which had a devastating effect on the Scavenger's systems.

With a faint whine of confusion it sank lifeless to the ground, its half-extended tentacles clattering limply on to the rocks. Cautiously, the Doctor turned round and pointed the sonic beam directly into the robot's domed casing for a few seconds.

'That should put you off the scent for the time being,' the Doctor murmured. Then taking out the ear-trumpet he applied it like a stethoscope to various points on the Scavenger's metal body. He listened with a smile of satisfaction to the silence within.

'That's right, you just get some rest,' he whispered, giving the robot a gentle pat. 'You've had a very busy day.'

The Doctor blew on the piece of Terullian and waved it in the air to cool it. Just as he finished stowing everything away in his jacket, and prepared to climb the ramp into the Sontaran space-craft, a heavy but rapid tramping came from the open hatchway. The Doctor dived into cover behind the inert, mechanical octopus and waited. Seconds later, Styr stomped into view and paused at the top of the ramp, staring suspiciously at the de-activated Scavenger. He jabbed sharply at the controls on his belt. The robot did not react. With a roaring hiss, the Sontaran thundered down the ramp, moving far less sluggishly than before, the Doctor noted. It approached with strong, rapid movements.

'You've obviously had a good breakfast,' he thought, 'which is more than I have.'

Styr examined the lifeless tentacles, panting with anger and suspicion. He stamped over to the domed capsule and began opening various panels, searching for a fault in the mechanism. The Doctor shrank behind the Scavenger, straining his senses desperately to anticipate the Sontaran's movements so he could keep out of sight. The pungent chemical vapour of Styr's breath hung in the air, making the Doctor's eyes water. To his horror, he felt himself about to sneeze and frantically searched for his red and white spotted handkerchief. Then he realised that Styr had stopped moving; his breathing was suddenly quieter —as if he were listening for something.

Just as the Doctor sneezed, a furious shouting and screaming broke out in the direction of the flat rocks. The Doctor waited, his eyes shut and his face buried in his hat. To his relief, Styr's huge bulk juddered past his crouched figure and hurried away towards the commotion, gasping eagerly. Keeping well hidden, the Doctor scrambled up the craggy ridge overlooking the flat rocks, and followed Styr with his spyglass.

Vural lay flat on his back with limbs splayed out, manacled to an enormous horizontal slab. Krans and Erak stood flanking their Commander, each man tethered to the slab by his ankles. A thick bar of Terullian about two metres long lay across Vural's bared chest and Krans and Erak were each shackled by the wrists to opposite ends of the bar.

'Lucky for you we're tied like this,' Erak yelled down at his helpless superior.

'Yeah ... if we ever get out of this alive, I'm going to tear you apart with my bare hands,' Krans screamed with almost hysterical anger. Vural lay silently shaking his head from side to side as if in a trance, his eyes staring crazily around him.

The crewmen fell silent as Styr strode into the arena of flat stones, dictating rapidly into the microrecorder unit. 'Assessment Period Gamma ... Solar Interval Eleven ... Experiment One Zero Nine ...' he gasped, approaching them with a gleam of anticipation in his flaring eyes. 'Human Physical Resistance and Moral Strength ...'

'What are you up to, you over-bloated frog?' growled Krans as Styr began to adjust the controls on his belt.

The Sontaran's mouth parted in a grotesque grin. 'Your abuse is a manifestation of fear,' he gloated. 'The release of adrenalin will assist you to perform this test with optimum efficiency.'

'What test?' Erak demanded.

Styr came closer, drooling and snorting. 'The destruction of your Commander ...' he sneered.

Krans and Erak glanced down at the trembling Vural and then at each other.

'No chance,' Krans shouted, his big body taut with defiance, while Erak shook his head and stared back at the Sontaran.

Styr activated a switch with a jab of his thick talon. 'You have no choice ...' he retorted triumphantly.

The Terullian bar hummed and vibrated, and began to sink into Vural's flesh. Instinctively, Krans and Erak lifted it clear, gaping at Styr in amazement.

The Doctor peered down from the ridge focusing his telescope on the vibrating rod suspended threateningly above Vural's breastbone. 'The Sontaran version of Saw-The-Lady-In-Half,' he murmured grimly.

Styr uttered a guttural, croaking laugh, his features swelling and throbbing with pleasure. 'One hundred kilograms ...' he gasped, adjusting the switches again. The bar sank immediately into Vural's chest, visibly compressing the ribcage. The two Galsec crewmen struggled to raise it once more, their eyes fixed upon the humming metallic rod in disbelief.

'Excellent,' Styr hissed, jabbing at his controls. 'One hundred and seventy-five kilograms ...'

Vural uttered a piercing shriek as the bar crashed into his stomach. Styr shook with excitement.

Krans lifted his end of the bar just clear of Vural's abdomen, the powerful muscles swelling through his tattered spacesuit. Erak, the weaker of the two, struggled desperately to equalise at his end, but he could barely raise the bar more than a few centimetres. Vural flung his head from side to side in agony, straining to tear himself free from his metal bonds.

'Fascinating,' Styr murmured. 'Your victim has ruthlessly betrayed you—and yet you attempt to save his life.'

'Murderer ...' spat Krans, his eyes blazing at the furrowed, reptilian features of the torturer.

Once again, Styr increased the mass of the bar. 'Two hundred and fifty kilograms ...' he bellowed. Erak crumpled to his knees, dropping his end of the vibrating bar on to the edge of the slab. With a prodigious heave, Krans managed to shoulder the other end, relieving some of the pressure which threatened to crush Vural's chest as if it were an eggshell.

'Do not be too confident, human,' Styr warned as Krans continued to stare defiantly at him. 'The experiment has hardly begun ...'

At that moment the communicator bleeped shrilly at Styr's side. For a moment he hesitated. Then, with a rasp of fury, he de-activated the gravity bar and snatched up the receiver.

'Earth Survey ...' he snarled.

The Doctor scrambled swiftly down the ridge and tucked himself into a niche a few metres away from the exasperated Sontaran, who was speaking in hushed, confidential tones into the communicator. Stealthily, the Doctor poked his ear-trumpet through a small gap between the rocks and eavesdropped.

'...the Strategic Council is not satisfied with your explanations, Styr,' hissed the Controller's voice. 'No further delay will be tolerated.'

The Doctor saw Styr glance guiltily across at the tethered crewmen. 'Controller, there have been un-explained occurrences ...' Styr blustered in a subdued tone. 'The Scout Unit has been sabotaged ... I have yet to locate and investigate the two associates of the female human discovered in the vicinity of the Trans-mat Terminal ...'

The image of the Controller glowed with dis-pleasure. 'You have tried our patience to the utmost, Styr. The Council requires your data—correctly en-coded—for immediate input. You must know that rendezvous with the Allied Squadrons from Hyperion Sigma is overdue by several Solar Intervals ...'

The Doctor's eyes widened as he listened to the Sontaran's secretive communication.

'...the entire galaxy must be in our control within the projected period ...' the Controller concluded.

'So *that's* what it's all about!' the Doctor breathed, slipping silently away and making towards the ravine where he had left Harry earlier. As he loped along, a daring and heroic scheme began to take shape in his mind.

Styr thrust the communicator into its holder and stamped back to his exhausted victims, his features puffed and twisted with cruelty and revenge.

Painfully, Harry groped his way back to consciousness. His eyes gradually focused on a blurred form looking down at him. With a sudden gasp of panic he flung out his hands and tried to roll away from the apparition.

'Easy now, easy ...' murmured a soothing voice. 'Everything's all right ... you're quite safe now ...'

Harry rested his throbbing head against something soft and comforting. Sarah's anxious face was bending over him. Warily Harry stared at the smiling, familiar, freckled features.

'Is ... is it really you, Sarah?' he muttered at last.

Sarah nodded happily. 'Yes, of course it is,' she replied.

Then everything came pulsing back into Harry's aching head. He tried to sit up, and fell back with a groan on to Sarah's folded anorak.

'Easy does it,' Sarah murmured. 'You've had quite a shock.'

'But why ... why did you attack me, old thing?' Harry said, wincing.

'Harry, I've told you before,' Sarah scolded gently, 'I am not a *thing*.'

'I don't know what you are ... I mean *were* ...' Harry mumbled with a grieved expression. 'But you certainly scared the wits out of me.'

'But I didn't attack you, Harry,' Sarah frowned. 'I think I must have fainted for a while, and then when

94

I came to I heard someone coming. I thought it might be that Linx creature—or whatever he calls himself now—so I hid. But it turned out to be you, Harry,' Sarah concluded, 'so I came out of hiding—and then you went bananas.'

Harry stared at Sarah open-mouthed. '*I* went bananas ... ?' he protested. 'I like that: you came at me like some demented ...' Harry broke off as he caught sight of the twisted circuitry hanging out of the surrounding rock. 'What on earth is all this?' he cried, hauling himself to his feet and going over to examine it.

Sarah shrugged. 'I haven't a clue,' she said. 'But whatever it is, it gave me some awful nightmares. I hope I'll be able to recall them when I'm writing my next feature article,' she added with a shudder.

'Well, I'm not likely to forget what just happened to *me*,' Harry muttered.

'You can tell a great deal from people's dreams,' cried the Doctor, sweeping into the alcove with scarf-ends flying. 'All kinds of things that they are not even aware of themselves ... Ah, Sarah Jane Smith ...' He smiled, gallantly doffing his hat. 'How lovely to see you up and about again—I do hope that Lieutenant Sullivan has been looking after you ...'

Harry looked exceedingly uncomfortable. Sarah ran over and gave the Doctor a delighted hug.

The Doctor looked at them with sudden seriousness. 'We cannot afford any more mishaps,' he said sternly. 'We've got an invasion on our hands.'

'An invasion?' Sarah cried, glancing round at the

bleak, towering rocks. 'There doesn't seem to be very much worth invading here ...'

'My dear Sarah—an entire galaxy,' the Doctor retorted, 'and we must do all we can to prevent it happening.'

'So the Sontarans *are* after Terullian deposits, Doctor,' Harry exclaimed.

The Doctor shook his head. 'I don't think so, Harry,' he replied. 'I have an idea that they are intending to establish a vast colony in this galaxy in alliance with the Hyperioi.'

'What are *they*? Sarah demanded sceptically.

'Another clone species,' the Doctor murmured, 'from a planet in Hyperion Sigma.'

'What chance do we have against two armies of clones?' Harry objected.

The Doctor took Sarah and Harry by the arm and began to outline his plan of action.

'The Sontarans are rigidly methodical creatures,' he explained, 'and if we can destroy Styr, there is every likelihood that the Alliance will withdraw for the present: at least until they discover what went wrong.'

'How are we going to destroy Styr?' demanded Sarah with an incredulous air.

The Doctor drew himself up to his full height and struck an imposing attitude. 'I intend to take him on in single combat,' he announced.

For a moment no one spoke.

'You *what*?' gasped Harry, exchanging glances of amazement with Sarah Jane.

'Yes. It's the only way,' the Doctor continued cheerfully. 'It is my guess that Styr will not be able to resist a challenge like that.'

'He'll murder you,' cried Sarah after another shocked silence. 'You'll just be torn apart ...'

'Oh, I don't think so, Sarah,' replied the Doctor with a brief, enigmatic smile. 'Styr's not accustomed to Earth gravity: for all his power he is pretty unwieldy. He has to return to his craft in order to re-energise himself at frequent intervals.' The Doctor poked Harry gently in the ribs. 'And that is where *you* come in,' he murmured mysteriously.

Harry gave a flattered smile.

'I do?' he said. The smile faded, and Harry looked apprehensive.

'Into the space-craft to be precise,' nodded the Doctor. 'If I can exhaust Styr, and force him to retreat to the ship for re-charging—well, we've got him, haven't we?'

'Have we?' chorused his nonplussed companions.

The Doctor linked arms with them and strode briskly out of the crevasse and into the ravine which led towards the hollow landing area. As they hurried along, he outlined his audacious plan ...

Erak had collapsed utterly exhausted among the rocks. Krans struggled alone, his heart bursting with effort, and tried to prevent the Terullian bar from completely crushing Vural. Styr loomed over the semiconscious Galsec Commander with his talons hovering near the array of touch-buttons mounted on his belt. He had decided to use his victims not only for the pleasure of torturing them, but also in order to extract information about the unidentified strangers, two of whom had so far eluded his grasp. The Sontaran realised the seriousness of his own position should the invasion be disrupted as a result of their activities.

'Why did you release the tall human?' he bellowed down at Vural, thick oily bubbles foaming around his lipless jaws.

The Galsec leader was silent, his face bathed in sweat, his eyes rolling.

'Three hundred kilograms ...' Styr gasped. Krans fought the crippling load of the bar on his shoulders. Just a few more kilograms and he knew he could not prevent it from sinking down and crushing Vural's chest.

Styr frothed with anger. 'I ask you for the last time,' he shrieked, 'what pact did you make with the tall stranger and his associates?'

'We have no pact ...' rang a sonorous voice, echoing round the craggy ridges.

With a hiss, Styr wheeled round. Astride a promontory of rock above him stood the Doctor, his scarf streaming dramatically in the wind.

'Aaaaaaaaagh ...' Styr breathed, his limbs beginning to jerk in anticipation. 'At last ...'

'Why waste your time with riff-raff?' the Doctor shouted, gesturing towards the three crewmen. 'These puny creatures you are so busy "assessing" are not

98

warriors, Styr. Why don't you fight someone your own size?' The Doctor snatched off his hat and brandished it with a proud flourish. 'I represent the true Human Warrior Class,' he challenged. 'Assess me if you dare ...'

With a roar of fury, the black vapour streaming from his nostrils, Styr raised his huge arm with its concealed weapon.

The Doctor gave a scornful laugh. 'Is that the Sontaran way?' he scoffed. 'The invincible warrior cowering behind a weapon ... ?'

Styr lowered his arm and hesitated. The Doctor jumped down on to a lower ledge of rock, still flourishing his hat. 'I challenge you, Styr,' he called. 'Single combat. Or are you afraid?'

Styr stretched out his enormous arms like a vice. 'Come then ...' he bellowed. 'Come to your death.'

Nimbly, the Doctor scrambled down the ridge, keeping up his repartee as he hopped from rock to rock.

'Oh, you can't afford to kill me, Styr,' he taunted, 'not yet—I know too much about your project ... and why it cannot possibly succeed.'

Styr waited for the Doctor to descend, his swollen bulk quivering with impatience, his talons grasping the air and the treacly saliva trickling down his suit, where it congealed in steaming blobs.

'Whatever you know, you will tell me,' he hissed. 'Everything—before you perish ...'

From her hiding place among the scattered slabs, Sarah waited for the coming struggle with sinking heart. She had done her best to dissuade the Doctor from taking such a terrible risk, but all in vain. She did not see how he could possibly survive, and clasping her hands to her mouth, she peered out anxiously into the arena as the two contestants slowly approached each other.

7

Duel to the Death

Harry edged his way nervously past the inert Scavenger—which resembled a giant crab stranded by the tide—and crept warily up the ramp towards the open hatch in the side of the Sontaran space-craft. His wellingtons squeaked noisily against the steeply inclined metal grid, and he kept glancing back to make sure that the robot had not stirred.

'I hope the Doctor's right about Styr being on his own,' he murmured as he summoned all his courage and stepped through into the faintly glowing interior of the space-craft. Low buzzing and humming sounds filled the air, which was warm and oppressively stuffy.

'I wonder what kind of atmosphere Sontarans usually breathe ... ?' he murmured, feeling suddenly faint and rather sick.

Harry tried to concentrate on the long string of instructions the Doctor had given him before they split up. The space-craft seemed to be composed of a kind of honeycomb of modules—each about the shape and size of a small, spherical room and all interconnected—with a larger central chamber entered by a series of curving passageways. Harry knew that he must eventually penetrate right to the central module to complete his dangerous and vital task; but first he must perform some preliminary operations—all in the correct order.

He turned to the left and began to clamber through the modules, squeezing himself through the small circular ports connecting each one to its neighbour. The walls of the tiny cells were covered in panels of unfamiliar-looking instruments which radiated an eerie, multicoloured haze as they flashed and clicked and buzzed to themselves.

'I wonder how Humpty Dumpty manages to move around inside this little lot ...' Harry frowned, as he counted his right and left turns through the linked modules, hoping that he was taking the correct route.

His query was soon resolved: within a few seconds he discovered that this section of the Sontaran spacecraft was inhabited not by Styr, but by a quite different creature. He became aware of a bright greenish glow, and a familiar humming sound coming from the cell ahead. Cautiously, he peeped through the circular port. There, its tentacles plugged in to various terminals in the curved wall, its electronic brain chattering away, hovered a miniature version of the Scavenger—its domed body a little larger than a football.

He watched, open-mouthed, as the tiny robot withdrew its probes with a series of snaps, revolved on its axis and quietly glided towards him ...

Springing lightly down from a ledge, the Doctor landed a few paces in front of his massive adversary.

He put up his guard like an old-fashioned pugilist, and danced nimbly from foot to foot, swinging first towards, then away from Styr with provocative ease as he circled slowly round him. The Sontaran began to lash out, his heavy arms slicing through the air with surprising speed. The bristling talons just missed the Doctor's head as he leaped backwards, a broad grin on his face.

With a menacing grunt, Styr lunged forward. The Doctor was enveloped in a cloud of sickening vapour, and he staggered back against a low slab of rock, coughing and choking. From her hiding place, Sarah gasped in dismay as the Doctor toppled and lay spread-eagled before the advancing Sontaran. With a gurgle of triumph Styr raised both arms and brought them down with the force of a pile-driver. In the nick of time, the Doctor twisted aside and Styr's talons smashed into the slab—sending sharp splinters of rock in all directions. Again and again Styr slashed down at his opponent, and each time the Doctor rolled aside. Sarah winced as Styr's powerful talons crashed against the hard rock, the impact echoing round the crags like gunfire.

'Stalemate!' the Doctor suddenly cried, rolling right off the slab and landing on his feet in a single, swift movement. With raucous gasps of frustration, Styr advanced on the Doctor like a tank.

'Now you will yield ...' he breathed, his talons snapping murderously and his vicious teeth glinting. The Doctor deftly wound a length of his scarf round his nose and mouth to help protect him from the

Sontaran's poisonous breath which hung in sticky clouds around them. With tireless ingenuity, he led the lumbering Alien all over the arena of fallen slabs, cleverly feinting aside or darting through narrow gaps whenever the clumsy Sontaran got too near him. Styr pursued him relentlessly, gradually exhausting his limited charge of energy.

Just as the Doctor sprang behind the enormous slab where the Galsec crewmen were tethered, something jumped out of one of his pockets and clattered among the boulders.

'Doctor ... the sonic screwdriver ...' Sarah cried in panic.

The Doctor shook his head emphatically, without taking his eyes off the approaching Styr. 'I can't use that, Sarah,' he cried through the woollen mask. 'It's against the Geneva Convention ...' and he gave a long, taunting chuckle which made Styr hiss with fury as he grasped Erak's end of the Terullian gravity bar and wrenched it free.

The tethers snapped like threads as Styr swung the bar from Krans's shoulder. The exhausted crewman pitched forward on to Vural in a dead faint. Styr whirled the vibrating bar around his head as if it were just a broomstick.

'Three hundred kilograms ...' he bellowed, as the bar buzzed through the air a few centimetres from the Doctor's skull.

'Very impressive ...' the Doctor murmured, choosing his moment carefully. Then, diving across the slab in a flying tackle, he grasped Styr's thick waist.

Clinging on for all he was worth as the Sontaran stamped about trying to shake him off, the Doctor quickly worked his way round so that he was behind his lumbering opponent. He fumbled among the cluster of controls set into the front of Styr's belt, and with a sharp jerk, altered the setting of the gravity bar switches.

Styr stopped moving, as if rooted like a tree. The free end of the Terullian bar crashed to the ground; then the other end slowly slipped out of Styr's fierce grip and crunched on to his broad elephantine boot. He uttered a thunderous roar of pain. The Doctor abruptly turned the switches in the opposite direction and, diving between the Sontaran's quivering legs, he snatched up the Terullian bar without any apparent effort. Before Styr could react, the Doctor brought the bar down with all his strength on to the back of the Sontaran's neck—just at the point where a small vent was inserted into the collar.

For a few seconds Styr was completely immobilised. His huge limbs stuck out rigidly at bizarre angles, his vast lungs stopped working and his glowing eyes went dim. The Doctor made the most of his momentary advantage, smashing at the section of Styr's arm which contained the hidden weapon, and at the instrument panels along his belt. Vivid sparks crackled as the Doctor rapidly wrecked the Sontaran's armoury of controls.

Without warning, a series of gigantic spasms shook the Alien's colossal frame. The rubbery lungs resumed their steam-hammer beating and the eyes burned like coals as Styr started forward, grabbing at the flailing gravity bar which the Doctor kept just out of his reach as he hopped from rock to rock up towards the ridge.

Sarah had emerged from her niche among the rocks, and was watching, heart in mouth, as the Doctor backed up the narrow ridge, forcing the gradually weakening Styr to flounder in pursuit. She knew that the Doctor could not possibly keep up his dangerous tactics much longer. Unless Harry returned very soon with his mission accomplished, it seemed as if all would be lost. She could hardly bring herself to look as the Doctor leaped along the precipitous spine of rock, taunting the gasping Alien with the Terullian rod.

A moan from the semi-conscious Krans nearby prompted Sarah into action. She ran across and tugged at the thin strands of Terullian binding the three exhausted crewmen to the slab, but they could do little to help her in her frantic efforts to release them. Suddenly she thought of the sonic-screwdriver, and quickly located it between the rocks where it had fallen. Studying the familiar, but extremely dangerous instrument, Sarah tried to remember how the Doctor operated it—she had watched him many times, but knew that the slightest mistake could be fatal.

Sarah set the combination switches along the handle to what she thought would be low power, and directed the transmitter probe at the point where one of Vural's manacles was fused into the slab.

'What is that thing?' muttered Krans suspiciously, too weak to restrain her.

'It's perfectly all right,' Sarah assured him. 'Now just relax ...' she said, turning to the pale and shivering Vural.

Sarah pressed the trigger button. Her arms began to shake as bursts of extremely low-frequency sound pulsed out in a tightly focused beam. For a while nothing happened. Sarah gritted her teeth and clutched the throbbing device to prevent it from jumping out of her hands.

Suddenly, the rock surrounding the end of the Terullian strand seemed to soften like toffee.

'Pull now,' Sarah cried.

Vural strained at the wire as hard as he could. To everyone's astonishment it sprang free, and Vural's arm was released.

At once, Sarah set to work to free Vural's other wrist.

'You're ... you're quite a girl ...' Krans muttered, when after a few minutes, Vural pulled his other arm away from the slab.

'Thank you,' Sarah said curtly, frowning with concentration. 'Perhaps you will now believe that we are your friends,' she added.

A desperate cry from the ridge made her glance up from her task. The Doctor's foot had caught in a crack and he was lying flat on his back, fighting off the advancing Styr with the gravity bar.

Just as Vural's last shackle broke free, Styr wrested the Terullian bar from the Doctor, and raised it high above his head like an axe. With a hoarse scream of hatred and revenge, the Galsec Commander forced himself to his feet and began to stumble up the rocks towards the ridge. Styr turned and watched Vural's screaming, hysterical figure stagger painfully towards him. Behind him, the Doctor struggled to free his foot from the crevice.

Styr waited, motionless, until the raging Vural reached him and began a pathetic attack. He allowed Vural to snatch the gravity bar and to strike him with feeble, harmless blows. Then, with a sudden burst of cruel amusement, the Sontaran lurched forward and knocked the helpless crewman off the ridge with a single sweep of his huge arm. Vural's screams died abruptly as he crashed lifeless into the ravine.

The Doctor managed to wrench his foot free just as Styr wheeled round on him again, his eyes roaring like blow-torches and the thick, black vapour jetting in hissing spurts from his swelling nostrils.

'And now ... you,' Styr gasped, reaching down and picking the Doctor up by the lapels of his jacket, as if he were a sack.

'You need a rest, Styr,' the Doctor murmured, his face only centimetres from the Sontaran's hideous, dribbling jaws and razor-sharp teeth. 'You don't look at all well to me.'

The Sontaran's flaring eyes bore into the Doctor's face. 'What is your function here on Earth?' he gasped, shaking the Doctor like a rag doll.

'Nothing much,' the Doctor replied in a choking voice. 'I just popped in to help a few friends from the Terra Nova ...'

'Terra Nova?' Styr panted. There was a tearing

sound as his talons pierced through the Doctor's coat. Helplessly, the Doctor hung like a carcass from a butcher's hook, racking his brains for some way of fighting back.

Styr shook him again and drew him even closer to his wobbling mask of a face. 'You will tell me all you know about the project ...' he hissed.

The Doctor grinned weakly. 'If I could only consult my diary, I could look it all up and tell you exactly what's going to happen,' he gasped.

With an enraged bellow, Styr swung the Doctor into the air above his head. 'Your absurd riddles are a pathetic attempt to gain time,' he roared.

The Doctor twisted his head round so that he could whisper directly into Styr's ear. 'I find time so useful,' he breathed, thankful for the relief from being throttled by his own collar. 'And from what I hear,' he went on, 'time is something that you and your Strategic Council are rather short of just now ... and it may be that I can help ...'

Styr hesitated. He was heaving with the effort of supporting the Doctor's weight, severely weakened by the unaccustomed effects of Earth's gravity, and by his attempts to catch the Doctor in the rugged terrain.

Meanwhile, the Doctor had been secretly feeling in his jacket, while whispering intently into Styr's ear in order to distract the Alien. He sneaked out a small pocket flask, uncorked it, sniffed briefly at the contents, and then reached across and tipped the flask upside down into the vent at the back of the unsuspecting Sontaran's collar. When the flask was empty, the Doctor re-corked it and thrust it back into his pocket.

Finally Styr lost patience. He whirled the Doctor round in the air and shook him over the sheer drop into the ravine.

'For the last time,' he roared. 'You will tell me the truth ... or you will perish ...'

Styr's words dissolved abruptly into a harsh torrent of black smoke and steam which gushed out of the vent behind his shoulders and from his mouth and nostrils. He stamped about on the narrow ridge, gasping and roaring. With a sudden shrug, he sent the helpless Doctor flying into the ravine.

Sarah crouched by the slab, staring up at the ridge in horror as Styr began to lurch down the slope towards his space-craft, his bulky limbs twitching spasmodically and dense smoke pouring out from all over his huge body. She shook her head slowly in disbelief, and gradually her eyes filled with tears.

'Doctor ...' Sarah murmured, 'Oh, Doctor ...'

Harry shrank back behind the ring-shaped bulkhead which surrounded the communication port joining the two modules, and made himself as small as he could. He watched with bated breath as the little spherical robot glided past him, its tiny scanner sweeping from side to side. It buzzed into the centre of the chamber where he was crouching and paused, its circuits working busily as it scanned the mass of instruments covering the walls. Harry jumped when

110

a thin probe shot out from the capsule and operated a row of contact buttons. But then the probe was retracted, and the miniature Scavenger hummed on its way into the next module.

Amazed at his narrow escape, Harry waited until the robot had gone and then clambered cautiously into the module ahead of him. Following the Doctor's instructions as best he could, he selected a sequence of coloured keys set into the panelling and turned them slowly in what he hoped was the correct order. Nothing seemed to happen.

'So far so good,' he muttered, wiping the sweat from his eyes and licking his dry lips nervously.

He worked his way through a series of modules which grew progressively larger, stopping occasionally to make adjustments to the instruments in accordance with the Doctor's directions, and listening constantly for the robot.

Eventually Harry reached the very heart of the Sontaran space-craft: a dark spherical chamber about nine metres in diameter, almost completely filled by a broad cylindrical structure in the centre, that crackled and flashed with some prodigious source of energy.

'This must be it ...' Harry breathed, 'the Catalytic Energiser ...'

Slowly he advanced round the structure, searching the quivering, flickering array of instruments for the section he wanted.

Suddenly something loomed in the shadow of a deep, semi-circular alcove which ran the height of the structure. Harry all but jumped out of his boots as he distinguished the bulky figure of a Sontaran standing motionless with its back against the Energiser. Unable to move, Harry gaped at the massive, dark shape. Its eyes were two dull points glowing faintly and staring straight ahead. Its slow, deep breaths sounded like some vast and distant machine.

'I'm too late,' thought Harry, his heart sinking. 'Styr's beaten us to it ... there's nothing we can do now.'

Eventually he took a brave and careful step forward. Nothing happened. He took two more steps. Still nothing happened. Gradually he made his way round the chamber towards the tunnel leading to the hatch. All at once his heart leaped into his mouth. A second Sontaran stood exactly like the first, pressed into the shadows, with faintly glowing eyes and slow, mechanical breathing, connected to the Energiser by a thick tube inserted into the back of its collar. It too made no movement when Harry recovered himself and tiptoed past.

He heaved a sigh of relief when, a little further on, he came across a third niche in the Energiser Structure which was unoccupied. 'This must be Styr's...' he murmured. 'Perhaps we're going to make it after all ...' At once Harry set to work, feeling about in the darkness among the maze of unfamiliar gadgetry which cluttered the vacant recess. Every now and then, he listened to check the slow, regular breathing of the two dormant Sontarans nearby.

At last he found what he was looking for: a grid

of small pyramid-shaped keys arranged in a complex chequer-board pattern. The grid was coded with different colours, but in the gloom Harry could hardly make them out. Sweat began to trickle down inside his collar as he chose a key and slowly turned it. He repeated the operation with a second colour, desperately trying to remember the correct sequence which the Doctor had repeated to him over and over again. The keys were close together and very stiff. It seemed to Harry that it would take him hours to complete the task, and the Doctor's warning, that the slightest mistake would be fatal, nagged away at the back of his mind as he struggled in the darkness.

As he knelt there, straining to turn the keys with numb fingers, he felt the floor of the chamber suddenly start to vibrate beneath his knees. He froze, listening intently. A heavy, erratic tramping was coming nearer and nearer.

'Styr ...' he shivered, the sweat turning to ice on his forehead. Frantically he wrenched and twisted the last few keys, expecting at any moment to be engulfed in a gigantic explosion. The stumbling and gasping of the approaching Styr thundered and echoed through the honeycomb of chambers as Harry gripped the final key with all his strength and tried to turn it.

Very, very slowly the key began to give. Harry knew that he only had a few more seconds. There was a rapid series of clicks and the panel came away in his trembling hands. At the same instant, Styr burst into the chamber panting horribly in his struggle for survival. Harry scrambled to his feet clutching the panel to his chest, not knowing which way to run. He stared round in confusion at the series of identical modules surrounding the chamber. Styr was almost upon him. In desperation he pressed himself against the Energiser Structure and waited.

Styr thrashed blindly past him into the vacant niche. Harry forced himself to remain still until he heard the Sontaran activate the Energiser Unit, and connect himself to the Structure. Then he hurled himself across the chamber and into the access tunnel. As he ran round the curve towards the open hatch he was stopped short. An enormous, metallic 'spider' was silhouetted against the daylight, its gleaming legs fanned around the hatchway and its phosphorescent body quivering at the centre. Harry's escape was completely blocked.

Instinctively he raised the panel like a shield in front of him. The 'spider' turned its eye towards the panel, and then flicked it back to Harry's face, expanding its iris with a shrill whirr. Buzzing like an angry hornet, the thing drew in its tentacles. Harry dived sideways into the complex of modules. Weaving right and left he scrambled through the echoing maze, trying to shake off the swiftly pursuing robot . . .

He seemed to have failed after all, just when success was within reach.

8

A Surprise and a Triumph

Krans and Erak had recovered a little from their ordeal at the hands of the Sontaran, and while Sarah strove to release their shackled ankles with the sonic-screwdriver, they did their best to try and comfort her.

'That ravine's hundreds of metres deep,' murmured Krans gently, 'no one could survive that kind of fall.'

Erak patted Sarah's shoulder clumsily. 'He wouldn't have felt anything ...' he added.

Sarah shook her head, fighting back her tears as she concentrated on freeing Erak's leg.

'If only I knew how to use this thing properly ... perhaps I could have saved him,' she said, focusing the sonic beam.

'You're doing just fine, Sarah Jane,' Erak replied as his ankle was released from the loop of Terullian embedded in the slab.

'The Doctor was so kind and so gentle ...' Sarah whispered, 'and he never wanted to harm anyone or anything ...' She switched off the sonic beam and stared silently up at the ridge from which the Doctor had been hurled by the maddened Sontaran.

'Unfortunately, Sarah Jane,' began Erak, 'we live in a universe where that is not possible ...'

'The Doctor lived in a universe all of his own,' Sarah interrupted quietly.

'He certainly did, Sarah,' Krans grunted, nodding towards the strange device lying inert in her hand.

Sarah stood up decisively and faced the two Galsec crewmen who were still rather dazed and unsteady on their feet.

'Well, we've got to manage by ourselves now, haven't we?' she said firmly, with an air of authority, although in reality she had little idea what they could possibly do against Styr without the Doctor's help. 'I suggest that we all stick together and ...' She broke off in mid-sentence as an excited and urgent shouting came from the direction of the Sontaran space-craft. 'That's Harry ...' she cried, with a smile of relief.

'Who?' chorused the puzzled crewman.

'Never mind now,' Sarah cried, scrambling over the slab. 'Come on you two ...' and she set off at a furious pace over the boulders towards the centre of the hollow, the bewildered crewmen limping after her.

Harry tore headlong down the ramp from the space-craft still clutching the precious panel from the Energiser Structure tightly in his arms. Before he could stop himself, he tripped over the de-activated Scavenger's tentacles lying scattered at the foot of the ramp, and sprawled among them in a hopeless tangle. Seconds later the miniature robot buzzed out of the hatchway in pursuit and hovered, its scanner sweeping the area in front of the space-craft.

'Doctor ... Doctor ... Where are you ... Doctor?'

screamed the helpless Harry, completely at the mercy of the tiny robot. He struggled to disengage himself from the tangle of wires as the mechanical hornet buzzed ferociously towards him.

Just as Harry threw up his arms in a futile attempt to shield himself, there was a high-pitched whine which nearly burst his ear-drums. The robot stopped in mid-swoop and disintegrated into a cloud of small fragments which showered over him like hailstones.

Staggering to his feet in amazement, Harry saw the determined figure of Sarah Jane astride a rock, holding out the sonic-screwdriver with both hands at arm's length, her body still trembling from the sonic vibrations.

'Bullseye, old thing,' he waved, and scrambled towards her, flourishing the panel in triumph.

Seconds later, Sarah, Harry and the two Galsec crewmen were huddled together among the rocks at the foot of the ridge, staring out at the huge sphere glinting in the late evening sun. The successful completion of Harry's mission was totally overshadowed by the news of the Doctor's fate in the ravine. No one spoke as they watched and waited, to see what would happen.

A long time passed before they began to notice that the ground was trembling beneath them—as if some extinct volcano were gradually becoming active again and preparing to erupt.

'It is possible ...' Harry insisted, recalling the hot bubbling chambers he had discovered in the underground maze of tunnels.

'Look,' cried Sarah, suddenly pointing to the enormous globe: its whole surface was shuddering and bulging as if from some colossal pressure building up inside. Thin wisps of white vapour began to seep out all over the dimpled sphere, as if from thousands of small holes. As they watched, the vapour grew steadily thicker, and started to stream out in long, thin jets. The air surrounding the space-craft was crackling as if charged with some kind of static electricity, and the sphere began to swell and shake like a vast wobbling balloon.

'It's getting *bigger* . . .' Sarah cried incredulously.

'Of course it is,' bellowed a voice behind them, 'and if you don't come back out of the way at once you'll be . . .' The rest of the sentence was lost in a roaring wind which abruptly sprang up around them, swirling round the space-craft like a maelstrom.

The Doctor was standing astride the ridge above them, his scarf-ends streaming almost horizontally, clutching his hat to his head with both hands. Krans and Erak looked stunned. Sarah gaped, speechless, at the figure of the Doctor as if it were an apparition. She was unable to move.

'Come on . . . quick,' Harry yelled, grabbing her by the arm and starting to drag her up the steep slope towards the ridge. Krans and Erak followed close behind. As they climbed, with the gusting whirlwind tearing at their bodies and the rocks vibrating under them like a giant drum, Sarah Jane continued to stare disbelievingly at the figure silhouetted against the skyline, her lips silently forming the word 'Doctor . . .' over and over again. When they were about ten metres from the summit, a tremendous hissing and gasping which drowned the wind made them look back.

Styr stood in the hatchway of the space-craft, enveloped in smoke and sparks. His gigantic frame had doubled in size. His eyes were two roaring jets of fire —like blow-torches—and a thick oily froth poured from his cavernous, red mouth and flew sizzling through the shrieking air. His vicious talons made useless, crippled, grabbing gestures towards them as they scrambled up the last few metres and threw themselves face down on the ridge beside the Doctor, their arms covering their heads.

'It's all right,' the Doctor shouted, staring intently over the summit of the ridge and into the hollow below. 'You can all watch ... but keep well down.'

One by one his companions raised their heads and peered over. Styr had stopped at the foot of the ramp. He was now almost three times his original size, his vast body glowing white hot. They could almost feel the heat on their faces as he turned his roaring eyes upon them.

Sarah shuddered as she stared transfixed at the swelling monster. 'It's all gone wrong ... it's a mistake ...' she muttered. 'The Doctor's creating a giant ... it'll be unstoppable.' She tore her gaze away and glanced across at the Doctor. He was observing the fantastic scene below with an expression that was half frown, half smile. Sarah tried to scream something at him, but the wind snatched away her words. At last she caught the Doctor's eye. He gave the thumbs-up sign and nodded towards the hollow.

As Sarah turned back her head, the air was filled

with an extraordinary sound which began as a deafening roar, and was transformed into an unearthly sighing as it gradually became recognisable as speech, 'Huumaaans ... you caannot escaaaaa ...'

The whirlwind seemed to be sucked back into the Sontaran's massive, rubbery lungs. The five onlookers clung tightly to the rocks to prevent themselves from being drawn into the shrieking vortex spinning into Styr's gaping mouth. Before their astonished eyes, the Sontaran and his space-craft began to shrink like rapidly deflating balloons.

In less than a minute, all that remained of them was two congealed heaps of smouldering and wrinkled metal. A tall column of smoke hung over the debris, curling into the still and silent air.

After a long pause, the Doctor stood up. 'Congratulations, Harry,' he smiled. 'A highly successful experiment—and it was all thanks to you.'

'Don't tell me I actually managed to do something right for a change,' Harry muttered, embarrassed but pleased as well.

The Doctor pointed to the panel Harry was still clutching. 'My dear Lieutenant Sullivan, you stole the Catalyser Filter Programme,' the Doctor went on, grinning broadly at the blank looks of his four companions. 'You see, when Styr plugged himself in to re-energise, the Nucleo-Enzymosis Reactions were accelerated randomly, thus leading to a catastrophic hyper-expansion of the Metabolic Fields ... when this reached Criticality, the Molecular Structures could no longer support themselves ...'

'Absolutely,' Harry nodded, looking round at the others.

Sarah flung her arms round the Doctor and hugged him, her face one enormous and brilliant smile. 'Thank goodness you're safe, Doctor,' she cried.

The Doctor looked puzzled. 'Why shouldn't I be, Sarah?' he asked.

'That fall ...' Erak put in, indicating the deep ravine behind them.

'My fault entirely,' the Doctor grinned, taking out the empty hip-flask. 'I didn't pour Styr a generous enough dram.'

'A generous enough *what*?' said Sarah in amazement.

'Glenlivet,' replied the Doctor. 'Since Terullian dissolves in alcohol, I thought, why not? Shocking waste of good Scotch though it is.'

'You mean to say that you made Styr drunk?' Sarah asked with an incredulous chuckle.

'Well, a little tipsy, Sarah, and extremely uncomfortable,' the Doctor replied.

'But I still don't understand, Doctor,' Sarah continued, with a puzzled glance at the precipitous drop beside them. 'Why weren't you killed when Styr threw you into the ravine?'

'Yes, I thought you might be wondering about that,' the Doctor smiled. 'It was all thanks to this.' He rummaged in one of his inside pockets and carefully took out the small piece of Terullian alloy, gripping it tightly with both hands.

'*That*?' cried Sarah, frowning in disbelief. 'How on

earth could *that* have saved you?'

The Doctor grinned mischievously at the four sceptical faces around him, obviously relishing their confusion.

'This is a fragment of the Scavenger's levitation system,' he explained, 'which works on much the same principle as the gravity bar. Now, when I poured Styr that wee dram, a drop or two must have got into his control unit and, by a stroke of good fortune, reversed the polarity of the graviton fields in this little thing.'

The others stared blankly at the insignificant-looking scrap of metal the Doctor was holding up in front of them.

'So?' Sarah said, after a pause.

'Well, it's obvious,' cried the Doctor. 'This little fragment suddenly acquired an intense dislike for the Earth's gravitational attraction and did its best to escape. Since it was trapped in my pocket, it slowed me down—and broke my fall. Simple really.'

'Let's have a look,' Sarah demanded, after a stunned silence.

'Are you sure you want to, Sarah?' the Doctor warned. Sarah held out her hand. No sooner had the Doctor placed the scrap of Terullian carefully in Sarah's palm, than there was a flash and a sizzling as something flew past their faces.

'Where is it?' Sarah cried, staring at her empty hand.

The Doctor pointed up into the sky with a long, bony finger.

'Somewhere up there,' he laughed. 'But it's no good

looking for it now. It's gone for ever.'

The whole sky was aglow as the giant disc of the sun sank towards the horizon.

'Come along, everyone,' the Doctor called, setting off down the ridge at a cracking pace. 'How time flies: we must hurry...'

'What about this invasion that's supposed to be happening, Doctor?' Harry panted as he caught up.

'All in good time, Harry, all in good time,' the Doctor muttered as he forged ahead. Just as they reached the foot of the slope, Sarah suddenly stopped dead.

'Listen,' she shouted. Everybody halted. A faint but persistent bleeping was coming from among the boulders. The Doctor rushed over and searched the crevices. Eventually, he stood up, brandishing Styr's communicator set.

'They must have heard you, Harry,' he grinned.

The Sontaran Controller's raging features glowed brightly on the small display panel.

'Good evening,' said the Doctor good-humouredly. 'What can we do for you?'

The Controller uttered a series of hoarse, incomprehensible gasps, his domed head swelling and filling the panel.

'Who ... ?' he finally managed to blurt out.

'You're getting warm.' the Doctor grinned. 'But I am afraid your little project has no hope of success. I've had a look in my diary, and it would seem that your best time to invade the Central Milky Way will be in about—three centuries ago to be exact. Assuming, of course, that you don't get lost in the Magellanic Clouds. Cheerio.' The Doctor let the communicator slip from his fingers and smash onto the stones. ' "Brinkmanship" I think it's called,' he said, with a satisfied glance at his four companions. He set off again with long, loping strides. 'It'll soon be dark,' he called, 'we haven't much time ...'

When at last they reached the circle where the TARDIS had disappeared, the nine spheres were ablaze with the reflection of the setting sun hanging low in the deep indigo of the sky. Krans and Erak eyed the rudimentary Transmat Installation suspiciously while the Doctor rushed from sphere to sphere trying to complete his adjustments before darkness fell.

Eventually, the Doctor signalled to the others to stand well clear. They all stared anxiously into the centre of the circle and waited. The Doctor flitted from globe to globe, muttering furiously away to himself as he fiddled with the complex mechanisms inside them. At last he stood back with folded arms and stared intently into the circle like an expectant conjuror.

Nothing happened. The TARDIS failed to appear.

'It's no good,' the Doctor murmured, shaking his head and frowning at the nine blazing spheres. 'It is not going to work, I fear.'

Sarah looked around at the rapidly darkening, barren landscape, where thin gaseous mists were beginning to gather again.

'Whatever are we going to do without the TARDIS, Doctor?' she said quietly. The Doctor did not reply, but stood with bowed head, hands thrust deep into his pockets, lost in thought.

'You'd better come and join us in the cave,' Erak said after a long pause. 'We've got quite a store of provisions ... and now that there are only two of *us* left ...' He broke off and glanced across at Krans.

Krans nodded. 'You saved our lives,' he growled.

Sarah smiled gratefully and shook her head. 'Thank you, but we just have to get back to the Terra Nova,' she replied. 'Vira and her people are depending on us.'

At that moment the Doctor suddenly sprang into action. He grabbed the Catalyser Filter Programme Panel which was still tucked under Harry's arm. 'Just what I need,' he cried. 'Just as well you didn't throw it away, Harry.'

Harry looked disappointed. 'But I was going to put that on the mantelpiece next to all my rowing trophies...' he grumbled.

Sarah gave Harry a sharp prod. 'If we don't get the TARDIS back, Harry,' she hissed, 'you'll never see your precious knick-knacks again.'

The Doctor was kneeling among the reeds, busily connecting a bunch of wires he had pulled from inside one of the globes to a series of terminals protruding from the back of the Panel.

'Never throw *anything* away ...' he murmured as he sonic-soldered the connections. Then he became absorbed in re-setting selected keys among the grid of coloured pyramids covering the front of the Panel.

'What good is *this* going to do?' Harry demanded, staring down at the makeshift circuitry surrounding the Doctor.

'Never you mind, Harry,' the Doctor snapped. 'Just don't tread on it, that's all.'

After a few last adjustments, the Doctor sprang to his feet. 'Off we go,' he cried.

'But ... where's the TARDIS?' Sarah said.

The Doctor gave a dismissive wave, striding impatiently into the middle of the circle. 'It will have returned to the Terra Nova by now,' he said. 'I think I remembered to set the Boomerang Orientators before we left. If it gets lost it should go back to where it came from. Do come along, everyone.'

Sarah and Harry exchanged puzzled glances as they followed the Doctor into the circle.

'Are you sure you won't join us, my friends?' the Doctor called to the two Galsec crewmen who were lingering uncertainly at the edge of the circle.

'No thanks.' Erak waved. 'We'll wait until your satellite people get down here. We'll be OK.'

Krans spat into the reeds. 'Never did trust those contraptions, anyway ...' he muttered, glaring at the fiery globes of the Transmat.

The Doctor directed the sonic-screwdriver towards the mass of circuits he had just assembled. 'As you wish,' he called, 'But I advise you to stand well back. It should be all right ...' he said, pressing the trigger.

Sarah and Harry instantly disappeared.

'Yes ... it should be all right,' the Doctor smiled, abruptly disappearing himself. 'Though one can

126

never be absolutely certain ...' continued his disembodied voice from the now deserted circle.

Krans and Erak gaped in disbelief as the Doctor suddenly reappeared for a moment, his hat solemnly raised in farewell.

'...Can one?' he grinned, before just as suddenly disappearing again.

For a long time the two crewmen stood staring open-mouthed. But the circle remained empty in the gathering darkness ...